Sylvia's room was the first door at the top of the staircase. I knocked quietly. When there was no response, I knocked harder. *She must really be a sound sleeper.* I tried the door, but it was locked. I rushed downstairs, retrieved her room key, and glanced at my watch. If Sylvia hurried, she'd still have time to make the start of the tour. Arriving back at her door, I knocked again.

"Mrs. Porter, it's Kelly. The tour is starting in a couple of minutes." I got no response, so I unlocked the door and peeked in. Sylvia was sitting in front of her dressing table, her back to me.

I opened the door a little farther. "Mrs. Porter?" I stepped inside the room. In the filtered light from the curtained windows, Sylvia's image reflected in the mirror. Her eyes were closed, and her head rested on her shoulder. She must have dozed off before making it into bed for a nap.

My attention was drawn to a brooch on the left side of Sylvia's blouse as I approached her. I hadn't noticed it before. It was a lovely piece—a large egg-shaped pearl surrounded by a burst of red.

I touched Sylvia's shoulder. No response.

"Mrs. Porter?" I gently shook her.

Sylvia's head rolled forward and hung down. Her dangling hair covered the side of her face.

I gasped, and my heart began to pound. I looked more closely at her. The burst of red wasn't part of a pin—it was blood . . .

Books by Janet Finsilver

Murder at Redwood Cove

Murder at the Mansion

Published by Kensington Publishing Corporation

Murder at
the Mansion

Janet Finsilver

LYRICAL UNDERGROUND
Kensington Publishing Corp.
www.kensingtonbooks.com

LYRICAL UNDERGROUND BOOKS are published by

Kensington Publishing Corp.
119 West 40th Street
New York, NY 10018

All Kensington titles, imprints, and distributed lines are available at special quantity discounts for bulk purchases for sales promotion, premiums, fund-raising, educational, or institutional use.

Special book excerpts or customized printings can also be created to fit specific needs. For details, write or phone the office of the Kensington Sales Manager: Kensington Publishing Corp., 119 West 40th Street, New York, NY 10018. Attn. Sales Department. Phone: 1-800-221-2647.

Lyrical Underground and Lyrical Underground logo Reg. US Pat. & TM Off.

First Electronic Edition: June 2016
eISBN-13: 978-1-61650-931-6
eISBN-10: 1-61650-931-7

First Print Edition: June 2016
ISBN-13: 978-1-61650-932-3
ISBN-10: 1-61650-932-5

Printed in the United States of America

To E.J., my husband, for his patience and support.

ACKNOWLEDGMENTS

I want to thank my husband, E.J., for his understanding and support as I wrote this book. He did a wonderful job entertaining the dogs when they'd "knock at the door" asking me to come out and play with them. I am very fortunate to be part of a writing group with Colleen Casey, Staci McLaughlin, Ann Parker, Carole Price, and Penny Warner as members. I greatly appreciate all the feedback they gave me and the laughs we shared. Thanks to Lann Westbrook for reading the book and sharing her thoughts, and to Georgia Drake for her thoughtful input along the way. I value the contributions of Michael Grimes, who shared his knowledge of European mansions, and cookbook author Susan Powers, who provided me with helpful information and shared some of her raw food creations with me. I am grateful to have the opportunity to work with an outstanding agent, Dawn Dowdle, and a great editor, John Scognamiglio. Thank you all.

Chapter 1

As I straightened out the Jeep after rounding a long curve, Redwood Cove popped into view. White buildings, looking like small squares, dotted a grove of trees. An aquamarine Pacific Ocean crashed against rocky outcroppings on my left, spewing foam and creating swirling mists.

Redwood Cove. My new home.

Excitement pushed away the weariness of long driving hours from Wyoming. My heart beat faster and goose bumps rose on my arms.

My new home. I whispered it aloud.

My new job. I spoke it aloud.

Tiredness slipped away as my mind raced ahead. My foot remained steady on the gas pedal, remembering the horse trailer I pulled behind me, filled with my belongings. I turned off the song "Walking on Sunshine" playing on the radio, put the window down, and let the salty breath of the ocean pour in.

I visualized the business cards nestled in a leather case in my purse. RESORTS INTERNATIONAL in raised letters at the top. KELLY JACKSON, MANAGER, REDWOOD COVE BED-AND-BREAKFAST artfully displayed in the middle. The cards would rest on the engraved brass holder my boss, Michael Corrigan, had sent as a welcoming gift.

I turned off the highway and the steeple of Redwood Cove Bed-and-Breakfast stood out against the sky. As I pulled into the driveway of the B & B, I inhaled deeply, struck by the sheer beauty of the place as well as the intense sweet fragrance permeating the air. The brilliant array of flowers on the trellised vines created a kaleidoscope of color next to the elegant white sculpted pillars. Gingerbread trim adorned the two-story inn.

I drove to the back and pulled off to the side of the parking area by the garage. The back door of the inn burst open, and a ten-year-old boy bounded down the stairs, followed by a short, heavyset basset hound.

"Miss Kelly! Miss Kelly! Hi!" Tommy Rogers slid to a stop in front of me. "Welcome back." His tricolored hound, Fred, jumped up and down next to him, or at least as best he could. His upper torso could only clear the ground by a couple of inches.

I smiled. "Glad to be here, Tommy."

He flew by me with Fred at his heels and clambered onto the fender of the trailer. "Did you bring a horse? Did you? Did you?"

"No, sorry, Tommy. It's filled with my things."

Helen, Tommy's mother, had followed him outside. She wiped her hands on her apron and gave me a hug. "It's so good to have you back, Kelly."

I returned the embrace. She looked much better than the last time I saw her, with more color in her face and no longer gaunt and haggard looking.

"And it's wonderful to see you, Helen. And Tommy and Fred again, of course." I smiled at her. "I'm excited to hear how things are going."

"Why the horse trailer?"

"I decided this trailer was the easiest way for me to haul my stuff. My parents are going to come for a visit in a couple of months when the Wyoming weather at the ranch makes California sound good. They'll take it back with them then."

Tommy climbed down and petted Fred, who'd been unsuccessful at jumping up on the fender of the trailer.

"I didn't bring a horse, Tommy, but I do have my saddle. Would you like to see it?" The last time I'd been here, Diane at Redwood Cove Stable had offered to let me ride an Appaloosa, Nezi, when the horse was available. I intended to take her up on it.

"You bet."

I went over to the trailer, unlatched the tailgate, and placed it on the ground, forming a ramp. The saddle was on a wooden stand I'd secured to the wall. Tommy rushed into the trailer and began to trace the intricate tooled leather pattern with his fingers.

"I'll be doing some riding at a local stable," I told him. "It's nice to have my own saddle because the stirrups are adjusted for me and the seat fits." *And it's part of my family life I brought with me.*

"Cool. Did you bring your bridle?"

"No, the bits used on the bridles are specific to each horse's need. There are lots of different types."

Tommy reached out and touched my leather belt, with the gold-and-silver championship barrel racing buckle. "Wow." His eyes were wide.

I had never heard a one-syllable word sound so long as when Tommy uttered that word. I had wrapped the belt around the saddle horn at the last minute. It wasn't everyday wear, but I'd ridden with it for years and decided to bring it along.

Before I could explain, my attention was drawn away to the rattling engine of an approaching vehicle. I looked down the driveway as a faded blue Volkswagen bus approached.

I knew it well.

The vehicle parked at the back of the inn, and tall, lanky Daniel Stevens emerged, the newly appointed manager of Ridley House, a sister property. His daughter, Allie, appeared from around the back of the bus. They were father-daughter look-alikes with their straight blue-black hair, high cheekbones, and copper-hued skin.

Daniel gave me a quick, friendly hug. "It's good to have you back."

"I'm glad to be here."

Allie smiled. "Hi, Kelly."

Tommy called out, "Allie, come look at this cool saddle and belt."

She left to join him.

"How are the renovations coming?" I asked.

"Fine. They're on schedule," Daniel replied. "Should be done by the beginning of next week, and Redwood Cove B and B will be ready to open."

"Michael asked me to do an inventory of some historic items at a place called Redwood Heights and help out with a festival this weekend."

"He told me," Daniel said. "After acquiring Ridley House a couple of months ago, Michael decided to put Redwood Heights up for sale. It's a little different from his other properties," Daniel said.

A glance passed between Helen and Daniel.

What was that about?

"I've been helping with some repairs to get the place ready to sell," Daniel continued. "Michael's got an interested buyer. It's worked out well, since I've been overseeing the construction on all three places."

Helen chimed in. "I've been preparing the afternoon appetizers. Since I was available, it made sense to give the cook at the Heights a chance to have a vacation."

"What's the event this weekend?" I asked. "Michael said you'd fill me in."

"The whales migrate this time of year," Helen explained. "And there are some great whale watching opportunities. Communities up and down the coast host various events."

"What fun!"

"We call our festival Whale Frolic," Helen added. "There'll be a chowder contest and the inns around town will have wine and gourmet treats for people to enjoy. Redwood Heights will be one of the places participating. The money from ticket sales benefits the local hospital."

Daniel watched the kids happily chattering as they examined the saddle and the belt. "There's a social hour at five at Redwood Heights if you'd like to go tonight," he said. "That is, if you're not too tired."

"Sounds great. After all the sitting I've been doing, I'd enjoy some activity."

"We can introduce you to the manager, Margaret Hensley." He shot Helen another quick look.

What was going on between these two?

A creaking noise caused the three of us to look down the driveway. A large motor home was crawling toward us, rocking gently from side to side. It drove by and parked in front of my Jeep.

Pictures of two larger-than-life beagles covered the side of the RV. One of them wore a pink collar, the other one blue. The slogan emblazoned next to them read, "Bedbugs? Termites? If you've got 'em, they'll find 'em. Call on Jack and Jill. Get the four-legged pros on the job and have a restful sleep tonight." A phone number was underneath it.

"Daniel?" I turned and looked at him. "Is there something you haven't told me?"

Chapter 2

Daniel laughed. "No. There's nothing to worry about."

"What a relief!"

"That's Stephen, Gertie's son. He and his dog team checked the inn and didn't find anything. Before he could check the other buildings, he got called away on a bedbug emergency, but now he's back."

It was my turn to laugh. "A bedbug emergency. That's a new one for me."

"Tomorrow he's going to start work at Redwood Heights. He—"

A honking car horn interrupted him. We looked around. A gold vintage Mercedes sedan sailed by and floated to a stop. Hands waved from the four open windows.

The driver's door opened and a diminutive man in a tweed jacket and tan cap got out. He opened the back door, took the cane that was handed to him, and offered his arm to the occupant. A tiny woman emerged, her silver hair glinting in the sunlight. While this was happening, the other three passengers disembarked.

The group rushed toward me, all talking at once.

"Welcome back, Miss Kelly," Ivan's booming voice rang out.

Mary Rutledge said in her usual soft voice, "So wonderful to have you here."

There they were, the Silver Sentinels, each of them dear to my heart. The dapper Professor, no-nonsense Gertie with her cane, Mary carrying the ever-present container of goodies, and the Doblinksy brothers, Ivan and Rudy. Their monochromatic hair color ranged from the Professor's white to Rudy's steel gray. I wondered what the crime-solving group of senior citizens had been up to since I left. I looked forward to finding out.

"So lovely to see you again, my dear," the Professor said. He clasped my hand and gave it a soft squeeze.

He had informed me when I first met him his name was Herbert Winthrop, but he went by Professor, part of his inheritance from the time he taught at the University of California in Berkeley.

"Nice to see you, Professor." I returned his gentle pressure.

Mary pushed the plastic box she held into my hands. "Honey, I'm sure you're hungry after all the driving you've been doing. I made you some special treats."

The same mothering Mary—round features, plump cheeks. Always sure to have something sweet to share with others.

I lifted the lid and found my favorite cookies: giant chocolate chip. My mouth watered at their freshly baked smell.

"Thanks. I'm sure they'll be delicious as always." I put my arm around her shoulders and gave her a hug.

Bear-sized Ivan and his slightly built brother jostled each other as they came to greet me.

Ivan turned his fisherman's cap around and around in his hands. "We so happy you back." His Russian accent was heavy, but his meaning came through clearly. "And now you stay."

"Yes, Ivan, now I stay." I smiled at him. "I'm happy to be back, too."

Rudy gently patted my arm. "Now we are all together again."

The Sentinels had made me an honorary member during my previous stay at Redwood Cove when we worked a case together. "Yes, and I look forward to hearing what you've been doing."

"A bit of this and bit of that," the Professor said.

Gertrude Plumber, who preferred to be called Gertie, approached. The cane all but disappeared when I experienced the strength of her personality. "Smart bringing your stuff in a horse trailer. From your parents' ranch, I presume. Didn't have to rent anything."

"Right." When I had been given the manager's job at Redwood Cove B & B, they had all turned out to wish me well and a speedy return as I left for my parents' place to pack my things.

"I'd like you to meet my son, Stevie," Gertie said.

While we'd been talking, the man driving the motor home had joined the group. He stepped forward and stood next to his mother, making me think of Paul Bunyan and Tinker Bell. Only this Paul Bunyan wore a tie-dyed, waffle-knit long-sleeved top, faded jeans, and Birkenstocks. His receding hairline flowed into a head of gray hair, then into a long ponytail. The wire-rimmed glasses he wore framed a pair of the gentlest eyes I'd ever seen.

He gave me a little wave. "Hi there."

"Glad to meet you."

Mary beamed at me. "Sweetie, you must be tired, so we'll go. As soon as we heard you were here, we wanted to come and say hi." She turned to Helen, and her dimples came into view. "Thanks for calling. I activated our phone tree, and here we are."

Ah, yes, the wildfire communication system of the small community. Obviously it was alive and well.

"Stevie's birthday is tomorrow, and I'm having a party. We'd like you to join us," Gertie said.

"I'd love to. Thank you for the invitation."

"You're welcome. Seven o'clock. And, please, no gifts. I'm keeping this simple."

They all piled back into the car and left amid a chorus of goodbyes.

As things quieted, we became aware of howls from the motor home. Two dogs peered at us through a window.

"I'll let Jack and Jill out now and start checking the garage and work shed," Stevie said.

He walked over to his RV, opened the driver's side door, and out bounded two beagles. They were almost identical in markings, except that one had a pink collar and the other one blue.

"The pink collared one is Jill, the other one's Jack. Big surprise, I bet." He chuckled. "It's an easy way for people to tell them apart."

Allie and Tommy had gotten out of the horse trailer along with the basset hound. Jill ran over to Fred and immediately began making friends. Jack, ahead of her, stopped and turned around with a puzzled look on his face. Where was his partner?

Jack turned and hurried back. Suddenly Jill went into play pose. The dogs didn't move for a couple of seconds, and then they were off. Brown, white, and black spotted canines ran happily around in circles.

Doggie playtime always brought a grin to my face. Their wild abandon expressed sheer joy. It would be wonderful if humans could do it so easily.

"Jack and Jill, come." Stephen leashed his team as they skidded to a stop at his side. "Time for you to earn your kibble."

Tommy came over. "They're trained sniffers, right?"

Stevie laughed. "Yes. You could say that."

"Fred is, too. He was trained to detect cancer."

"Wow! I've heard about that," Stevie said. "They have a lot in common. Maybe that's why they're getting along so well."

Tommy looked at his mother. "Allie and I are going to start our homework now."

"Good idea. There's fresh lemonade in our refrigerator."

Tommy and Helen lived in a small cottage behind the B & B. He and Allie raced each other, with Fred close behind. It wasn't much of a match with Allie's long legs.

"Is it okay to pet your dogs?" I asked Stevie.

"Sure. They love all the attention they can get."

I knelt down next to them and rubbed their ears, one hand for Jack, the other for Jill.

Stevie turned to Daniel. "I'll check Helen's cottage tomorrow. I should be done by late morning, and then I can start on Redwood Heights."

"Great. I'll meet you here, and we can go over together."

"Sounds like a plan, man."

I stood. "Your dogs are sure cuties."

"Thanks. They're my kids. I love them. And they're good at what they do." Stevie led the beagles off to the garage.

Daniel moved toward the trailer. "Kelly, do you want help unpacking?"

"No, thanks. I'm just going to take in the basics I used at the hotels on the drive here for now."

Helen started back to the inn. "I need to finish the appetizers for tonight."

"Why don't I pick you both up in an hour?" Daniel asked.

Helen and I agreed that worked for us.

Looking around, I decided the best place to leave the trailer was next to the garage. I closed the horse trailer, drove it closer to the building, and parked. I unhitched it and took the Jeep back to the parking lot. I grabbed my backpack and black duffel bag from the backseat and went into the inn through the back door. I entered the large multipurpose room.

The kitchen area lined one wall, with a counter separating it from the main room. It worked as both a place to eat and a food preparation area. A granite island with stools to accommodate six people stood next to the counter. A large oak table supplied a place to sort papers, lay out numerous contracts, and provided an alternate eating site. A television, overstuffed chairs, and beanbags that could be pulled out for additional seating were off in one corner for leisure moments.

It was the main room for the inn's staff activities. The person who designed it had functionality and quality in mind. It was a room you walked into and felt surrounded by comfort. I loved it.

"Your place is open," Helen called out as she grabbed trays of stuffed mushrooms from the refrigerator.

"Thanks." My place. My wonderful, incredible place.

Once again my heart raced faster. This time my feet picked up their pace as well.

The Oriental runner covering the dark wood floor muffled my steps as I walked down the hallway. Ahead, I saw the door to my rooms. I paused a moment, then opened it.

As I stepped in, I thanked the architect who created the work of art that brought light and nature together in such a spectacular way. Walls of glass framed the rugged coastline. Churning waves, craggy rocks, and a jagged beach stretched out ahead of me. The inn's lush gardens enclosed the room on one side. The flowers created a riot of color and looked like a painting. Little brown birds—LBBs, as my birder friend called them—landed on a feeder in the yard, so close I could see the distinctive differences in their feather patterns.

I put my bags on the bench seat next to the wall and went into the miniature kitchen. It was as I remembered. Everything sized for a small unit, except for the large, professional coffeemaker, an important piece of equipment in my boss's life. I put the makings together for an espresso and started it up. I peeked in the bedroom and was surprised to see a new comforter set. Swirls of green and blue made it one with the view from the front room.

I pulled a small, buttery-soft leather pouch from my fleece pocket and traced the multicolored beads sewn in a V-shape on the front of it with my finger. I opened it and dropped its contents onto my palm. A miniature black raven looked up at me with its bright blue eye. I studied the meticulously carved, artfully sculpted wings and the lines of the feathers.

Grandpa had asked me to pick a Zuni fetish from his collection to accompany me on this new path in my life. It had been a difficult decision. Native American lore attributed different meanings to many animals. The badger had the ability to help reach a desired goal. I was excited about my new job and wanted this to be my career, so I was tempted to choose an amber one from the assortment. But I felt pulled to the raven, believed to give its keeper courage to work through problems and face personal fears. In the end I had settled on the black bird.

I put him on the table next to the bench seat, then curled up on the soft cushions and sipped the coffee. Daniel would be back soon, but I wanted a moment to soak this all in. It was a new beginning with wonderful friends already a part of it. Still hard to believe. I felt so lucky.

Looking at my watch, I saw it was time to move. I unpacked the heavy company fleece and the lightweight nylon jacket Corrigan had sent with the cardholder. They had REDWOOD COVE BED-AND-BREAKFAST embossed underneath RESORTS INTERNATIONAL. A glance outside showed fog beginning to swirl in. I chose the fleece.

I joined Helen in the main room.

"Ready to go?" Helen asked.

"Sure. What can I help you with?" Two boxes were on the counter, containing stacks of plastic-wrapped trays full of appetizers.

Through the back door window, I saw Daniel's bus roll into the backyard.

Helen pointed to a box. "Grab that one."

I could almost hear my red hair beginning to curl in the foggy air as I walked outside. I got in the middle bench seat and placed the hors d'oeuvres on my lap.

Redwood Heights was only a short distance from the Redwood Cove Bed-and-Breakfast. A block from the inn, we took a left turn down a hill and went around a corner, and there it was.

I gasped. The building sat nestled among giant redwoods. It was two stories with row after row of windows interspersed with French doors leading to balconies protected by black wrought-iron railings. A master craftsman had twisted them into intricate twirls and patterns, same as the ones encircling the top of the building. The mansion reminded me of a majestic English queen, the towering trees her staff-in-waiting, her billowing skirts the outcropping of buildings spreading to either side, her crown the widow's walk on top.

This answered one question—what Daniel and Helen had meant when they said this property was different. It definitely wasn't like any other Resorts International properties I knew. The ones I'd experienced and the ones I'd read about had a more casual air to them. We pulled into the back and unloaded. Helen busied herself in the kitchen, heating the appetizers.

"I get them ready, then the staff minds them and adds as necessary to the hot trays in the parlor," she explained.

"The guest area is this way." Daniel pointed to a hallway.

We walked into a room filled with guests and over to the sideboard holding the evening's offerings.

Large crystal chandeliers lit the room. Tables were covered with white brocade tablecloths. A stack of fine china plates sat next to an array of artisan cheeses and several wine choices.

I looked around the room. Lustrous pearls rested on cashmere sweaters. The diamond on one woman's hand competed in size with the crystal finial hanging from the center of the chandelier. The gentle orchestral strains of "Moon River" accompanied the conversation in the room.

These weren't the fleece-and-denim Redwood Cove visitors I had gotten to know. I straightened my jacket and ran my hand through my fog-frizzed hair.

A young woman offered some of Helen's appetizers to a guest. As she reached for one, a shrill scream ripped through the room, shattering the tranquil moment.

Chapter 3

The room went quiet, except for the music. People began to stand. Daniel and I rushed across the room.

"Please, everyone, remain seated," I said. "Let us see what's happened."

People sank back into their chairs.

I flung open the parlor door. The registration area was off to my left. A steep, wide staircase dominated the area ahead of me. A woman lay sobbing at the bottom of it in a crumpled heap.

I knelt beside her, and Daniel joined me. Tears had washed her artfully applied eyeliner down her cheeks, creating black rivulets through the powdered blush.

"Are you hurt?"

"I'm not sure," she said in a tremulous voice. "Someone . . . someone pushed me." She sat up and ran her fingers through her carefully coiffed blond hair, causing furrows in the heavily sprayed hairdo.

Daniel and I scanned the open landing above and saw no one.

"I'm Kelly Jackson, and this is Daniel Stevens. We work for Resorts International. Are you injured? Do we need to call a doctor?" I asked.

The woman slowly extended her arms, flexed her fingers, and then stretched each leg. "I feel sore, but I don't think anything is broken."

"I'm so glad to hear it," I said.

"I'm Sylvia Porter." The woman's voice quavered. She cast a frightened glance at the row of rooms above, then looked at us, her eyes wide with fear. "I could've been killed! You need to search and find who did it. They're hiding up there."

Daniel and I looked at each other.

Sylvia grabbed my arm. "Please, promise you'll search . . . that you'll find the person." Her nails dug into my flesh.

I put my hand on hers. "We'll do our best."

Daniel nodded in agreement.

A pair of very pointed black patent shoe tips appeared in my peripheral vision. I turned, and my gaze traveled up finely tailored women's black slacks and over a suit jacket. The woman's expression appeared more tolerant than concerned. Her short black hair completed the picture.

"Mrs. Porter, what's happened? Are you okay?" The woman bent over and patted Sylvia's shoulder. "There, there, dear. It looks like you've slipped and had a nasty fall."

"I didn't slip, Mrs. Hensley." A belligerent tone crept into Sylvia's voice. "I was pushed."

So this is the manager and the source of the exchanged looks between Helen and Daniel.

Sylvia looked at Daniel and me. "You believe me, don't you? I know the difference between slipping and being shoved." She threw a defiant glance at the woman bending over her.

"Do you think you can stand?" Daniel asked. "I'll help you."

Sylvia grabbed the ends of the staircase railing. Daniel put his hand under her arm and helped her slowly to stand. The sobs reduced to sniffles.

"Did you see who . . . pushed you?" the woman next to me asked.

"No, Mrs. Hensley. If I had, I would've told you." She glared at the manager.

"I'll let the guests know what's happened," Mrs. Hensley said, "and I'll have Tina go upstairs with you and see that you're comfortably settled in your room. She'll be happy to prepare a tray for you from the parlor."

"That would be nice." Sylvia took a tissue out of her pocket and dabbed under her eyes.

"And I'd like to offer you a complimentary bottle of wine for your stay here."

Sylvia shot a quick glance at the manager. "Well, I really enjoyed the Oak Tree merlot we had yesterday afternoon."

"Of course, Mrs. Porter." Hensley's eyelids dropped a fraction and her eyes narrowed. "You have excellent taste. I'll have it delivered to your room."

The manager disappeared into the parlor.

Sylvia looked at Daniel and then me. "You said you were going to search. You're going to do that, right?" Tears began to well up again.

"Yes, we gave you our word. We'll look," I replied.

Mrs. Hensley returned as Sylvia sagged against Daniel at our response. A young woman with short, brown curly hair came back with the manager.

"Mrs. Porter," the girl said, "I'm sorry you had a fall. Let me help." She supported Sylvia on one side, and Daniel supported on the other, and the group started a slow ascent up the wide staircase and into the woman's room.

I turned to the woman in black and held out my hand. "Kelly Jackson, manager at Redwood Cove Bed-and-Breakfast."

"Margaret Hensley." Her cold hand barely touched my palm.

I looked at the row of rooms above us through the second-floor railing. I counted six. "I think Daniel and I can do the search pretty quickly."

"There's no need. The woman tripped and fell. Plain and simple."

My shoulders tensed. "There is a need. We gave our word."

"It'll be a complete waste of time."

"Keeping one's word is never a waste of time." The heat of a blush started, an angry one. My mental mirror reflected my red-and-white-splotched face.

Our verbal swords were drawn and poised for battle.

After a short pause that seemed like an eternity, she said, "Fine." The word seemed to struggle to escape her clenched teeth. "Come with me."

She turned, and I followed. We entered a massive office with dark oak paneling. Hensley marched over to the wooden cupboard, pulled a key from her pocket, and opened it. Skeleton keys lined the back, each on a numbered peg. A large metal ring at the bottom held numerous keys.

The manager grabbed it and turned to me, thrusting the keys in my direction. "You'll find no one. The Porter woman has been a pain since the day she arrived. A first-class drama queen."

I took the keys. "Thank you." I turned and left, determined to engage as little as possible with the angry manager.

I met Daniel on the landing. "I think if we say we're housekeeping, that will be the easiest way to announce ourselves to see if there's a guest in the room."

"Good idea."

I knocked on the first door. "Housekeeping." I waited a moment, knocked again, and said, "Housekeeping."

When no one answered, I inserted the room key. The large metal keys were heavy and cumbersome. It took some jiggling to make the lock turn. I opened the door, and Daniel searched the closet, while I looked under the bed and behind a large, high-backed chair in a corner.

We didn't find anyone and left the room. It took a bit of work to lock the door. The authenticity of the metal key was nice, but right now a more modern system would be nice. I went to the next room.

"Daniel," I said, as I struggled with another recalcitrant lock and key, "why don't you search, and I'll go unlock the next room. When you come out, I'll lock it up. I think we can go faster that way."

"Sounds like a good plan."

With our new system, we made short work of the rest of the rooms.

The heavy keys dangled from my fingers. "I'll return these to Hensley."

"Okay. I'll meet you in the kitchen."

The office door was open. I knocked on the frame and walked in.

Hensley looked up from behind a large oak desk. "Did you find anyone?"

"No." I handed her the keys.

"Like I said, a waste of time." She put the keys in the cabinet and turned and looked at me. "Michael Corrigan informed me he assigned you to work here."

She didn't lose a beat as she shifted the subject. No matter. I'd had horses change their gait on me like this, and I'd been able to stay on for the ride.

"He asked me to do an inventory." *Not be your employee.*

Our eyes locked. Neither of us blinked. I was a champ at this. My brother James and I used to spar like this all the time.

The phone rang, ending the silent standoff.

Hensley answered it. "Of course, Mrs. Carter. I'd be happy to meet you and discuss dining options." She put the phone down and stood.

"The guests finish breakfast at about eight. I like to mingle with them." The manager grabbed a leather-bound notebook off of her desk. "Will nine tomorrow work for you to begin?"

For some reason it didn't sound like she was asking. "Fine."

"Tomorrow then," she said over her shoulder as she left.

I took a deep breath as I walked down the hallway. Now I knew what the other look meant between Helen and Daniel when they'd mentioned her name.

Daniel and the young woman from earlier stood next to the kitchen sink, talking. They stopped when I entered.

"Kelly, I'd like you to meet Tina."

She gave a little wave. "Hi. Nice to meet you."

"Same here."

"Helen walked back to get dinner started for her and Tommy. The trays are in the van," Tina said. She handed me a brochure. "This gives some of the history of Redwood Heights. I thought you might enjoy reading about it."

I took the pamphlet. "Thanks."

We took our leave. I sank back into the passenger seat, waves of tiredness threatening to drown me.

"Quite the end to a full day," Daniel said.

"Yes, and there's still the evening to go." I had told my boss I would call.

"Tina said all the guests were in the parlor when Mrs. Porter fell."

"Good to know. We did what we could. I doubt if we'll ever really know what happened."

We unloaded after the short drive to the inn. Daniel got Allie from where she was doing homework with Tommy, and they headed home. I walked into the workroom and relished its warmth after the cool ocean air.

Helen pulled a pan from the oven. "You must be exhausted."

"Yes, I am."

"I remembered how much you liked the first dinner I made for you, so I prepared the same one again."

Two pieces of oven-baked chicken covered with fresh chopped herbs sat next to bright green broccoli with a light covering of Parmesan. A mixture of brown rice and sautéed mushrooms completed the dinner. I knew most, if not all of it, was organic—and it smelled wonderful.

"Helen, that's very thoughtful of you." But not surprising, from what I knew about her. "I really appreciate it."

I carried the tray to my room and put it on the table in front of the window seat. I didn't want it to get cold, but I needed to call Corrigan. His hearty voice always gave me a shot of energy.

"Hey, Kelly, good to hear from you. I assume this means you made it okay."

"Yep. I've already reconnected with the Silver Sentinels and made it over to Redwood Heights. Quite the place."

"It's not the usual kind of place I purchase, but I heard some foreign investors were going to buy it and modernize it. I couldn't let that happen. Too much history there."

"I met Margaret Hensley." I stopped and waited for his response.

After a couple of seconds, he said, "She's an old friend of mine. The manager at the Heights asked for a leave of absence. Margaret wanted to get away for a while. She's dealing with . . . some problems."

I wondered what kind of problems. Something that made her especially curt?

"New York City to Mendocino might have been a bit too much of a planetary leap for her," Corrigan said.

That helped to explain the alienating attitude.

"I'll begin the inventory tomorrow."

"There's something else you need to know." Corrigan's deep sigh carried over the phone. "We've had a few pieces of jewelry stolen from some of the guest rooms."

"Oh, my gosh. Do you have any idea how the thief got in?"

"We're not sure. We called the police in, of course, but they found nothing. It hasn't been going on for very long and happens during the day. I want you to keep your eyes and ears open for anything unusual."

"Of course."

We talked about a few business details and said good night. I had just finished dinner when Helen called.

"Kelly, Deputy Sheriff Stanton's here. He has questions about what happened at the Heights."

"Okay. I'll be there in a couple of minutes." I put the dishes on the tray and headed for the multipurpose room.

The deputy, a tall, heavyset man, waited there.

"Deputy Sheriff Stanton," I said, "nice to see you again."

"Same here Ms. Jackson. I heard you got back today."

"What can I do for you, Deputy Sheriff?"

"I need to talk to you about what happened at the Heights today."

"Before you start, Bill, would you like some coffee?" Helen asked.

"Sure. The usual would be great."

Easy use of first names and the usual. Interesting.

"Kelly, anything for you?"

I put the tray on the counter. "No, I'm fine after the great meal you fixed."

The deputy accepted the coffee Helen handed him. "A woman staying at Redwood Heights called and reported an attack. She says someone might have tried to kill her. Said you were there."

"I was there, but I didn't see what happened." I filled him in with what I knew.

"Margaret Hensley's convinced Mrs. Porter tripped and fell. But the woman was adamant about feeling two hands at her back and being shoved."

"She didn't say anything to us about the hands."

"Okay. Thanks. Good to have you back."

I left Helen and the deputy sheriff talking and walked back to my room. Sylvia hadn't said anything about feeling someone's hands. Was she embellishing her story? Making it more believable? Or had someone really tried to hurt her . . . or to kill her?

Chapter 4

I woke before my alarm sounded the next morning and took a long stretch. My stiff muscles appreciated the movement. Days of driving and lack of normal activity had taken their toll. I punched the button down on the alarm and pulled the comforter up around my chin and sighed with pleasure. I was in my new home.

Excitement then spurred me out of bed. Slipping into my clothes and my black sheepskin slippers, I headed for the kitchen. The gleaming giant coffeemaker greeted me. I got it started and looked in the refrigerator. Helen's thoughtfulness showed. She'd stocked it with gleaming red apples, goat cheese, sparkling water, and milk. A note on the counter said bagels were in the freezer.

I grabbed a small bottle of water. While the coffee brewed, I went into the living room and peeked around the blinds. At six thirty in the morning, the night had only begun to recede, so I left the window covered. I sat on the bench seat and relished the thought of the day to come—my first full day as manager of Redwood Cove B & B. Not even the thought of working with Margaret Hensley dampened my spirits.

After pouring a cup of coffee, I took a quick shower and applied light makeup. I had only unpacked a couple of boxes of essentials last night. Black jeans, a green turtleneck, and a black company fleece vest provided my outfit for the day. I tidied the work folders I'd reviewed and put the Redwood Heights pamphlet on top of them. I'd enjoyed learning its history and that of its owners, the Brandons.

I shut the suite door and walked down the hall toward the workroom. The well-remembered smells of freshly baked pastries greeted me. As I entered the area, my eyes showed me what my nose already knew. Cooling racks held a variety of muffins and croissants.

"Good morning. How did you sleep?" Helen asked as she pulled strawberries out of the refrigerator.

"Like a cowboy after a long day riding fence." I stretched. "It's surprising how tiring just sitting and driving can be."

"It sounds like you slept well." Helen laughed. "But I'm not sure what that phrase means."

"One of the ranch chores involves riding the perimeter to check the fence for any breaks and repairing them. Those are long days in the saddle."

"I bet you're glad to have the trip behind you."

"Definitely."

Tommy burst into the room, Fred at his heels. He raced to the counter and jumped on a stool.

"Good morning, Miss Kelly."

Helen put a bowl of cereal piled high with blueberries, strawberries, and bananas in front of him and poured creamy milk on top. A breakfast sundae. She placed a stainless steel dog dish in the corner, and Fred got down to the business of eating his breakfast.

"Hi, Tommy, how are you today?" I asked.

"Great!" He shoveled a spoonful of cereal into his mouth. "Miss Kelly, you said horses had individual bits. I read about it last night. There are lots of types of bits. I learned about snaffles, curbs, pelhams—"

"Tommy, eat your breakfast," his mom said.

"Okay. Then there's the hackamore, which has no bit."

I laughed. "Very impressive, Tommy."

He hadn't changed since I'd seen him last. He was still the same walking, talking encyclopedia. By now, he might know more about bits than I did.

"Whoa, cowboy," Helen said. "It's time for you to finish eating and get to school."

"Okay, Mom." His shoulders drooped a little, but then he straightened up. "I have science club after school. We're building a rocket!"

"Sounds like fun," I said.

"Yeah, it is." He finished his last bite of cereal, gave Fred a hug, and grabbed his backpack.

"Tommy, remember you need to be home by five."

"Okay, Mom." He turned to me. "See you later, Miss Kelly."

"Bye, Tommy."

He stopped at the door. "Oh, and our core class gets to go on a field trip today to watch whales."

"Okay, Son. Now scoot."

Off he went.

Fred sauntered over to his bed and flopped down with a grunt.

"The science club seems to have him excited."

"Yes, he really enjoys it, and he's finally made some friends."

"How's his Asperger's?"

"They did some testing, and it's still considered a mild case."

"Great news." I stood. "Right now, I'd better get to Redwood Heights."

Helen nodded toward some baskets. "As soon as I finish those, I'll be going there myself. They're late morning snacks for the whale watching group."

"See you later."

I walked back to my room, thinking about Tommy. He'd had a hard time here. Having Asperger's and being the new kid in a tight-knit community had been very difficult. It sounded as if things were changing for the better.

I put my fog-permed hair into a clip, taming my Orphan Annie look, and slipped on my down parka. I'd been fooled before by thinking all of California was warm and sunny. The cold, moist ocean air on the northern coast cut right through you.

Walking to the mansion was exhilarating. The ocean crashed and boomed to my left. I inhaled the salty air. The large building loomed ahead, the towering redwoods surrounding it even more impressive than yesterday as I approached on foot. Impressive and somewhat oppressive.

I entered through the front door and walked into the main entryway, where Sylvia had fallen. Spying a coatrack behind the reception desk, I slipped out of my jacket and hung it up. Continuing down the hallway, I peeked in Hensley's office. She was sitting behind her massive desk, a row of neat stacks of papers in front of her.

"Good morning," I said.

She looked at me over the top of red-rimmed reading glasses. "Hello," she replied.

"Where would you like me to start the inventory?"

"In the parlor, but first I'd like to show you the safe where the keys are kept for the cabinets and the carriage house."

Hensley gave me the combination and showed me how to work it, explaining there were two keys for each door. A key for the cabinet housing the guest room keys was in there as well.

She handed me two keys. "These will get you started." The carriage house key was a large, metal skeleton key. The new, smaller one unlocked a cabinet in the parlor.

"About yesterday"—Hensley paused—"I feel we got off on the wrong foot. That Porter woman pushes me to my limits."

The phone rang, and Hensley punched a button. "Yes?" She listened for a couple of seconds. "I see. Call me later in the day to let me know how you're doing." She hung up and looked at me. "I need you to go with the guests today . . ." She stopped as her gaze drifted to the manager logo on my fleece. She cleared her throat. "How would you like to go with the whale watching tour?"

"Sure. What's up?"

"Tina Smith, the staff member you met yesterday, was scheduled to escort the group. She's ill." Hensley frowned. "Not for the first time, I might add."

"Sounds like fun. I'd be happy to do it." Whale watching and growing up in Wyoming didn't exactly go together. This would be a new experience.

"The tour leaves in fifteen minutes. The group meets out front." She handed me a list of names. "Claude Baxter, a local chef we hire part-time, will meet you there. He grew up in the area and assists with some of our tours, as well as preparing special meals for our guests. He'll help during the whale watching and then preside over a gourmet lunch we've arranged for our guests. I always send two people so if there's a problem one can deal with it while the other one stays with the group. It's a lot of staff for only twelve people, but this is a luxury resort and catering to our clients' needs is a priority."

I retrieved my jacket and joined the guests in the driveway as three massive black Cadillac Escalades rolled up. Sylvia Porter mingled with the group.

I approached her. "Mrs. Porter, how are you feeling today?"

"Much better," she said, sniffing.

A tall, lanky man stepped out of the first vehicle and addressed the group. "I'm Ben," his soft voice drawled. "I'll be one of your guides today. There'll be four people to a vehicle."

The drivers of the other two SUVs joined him.

Sylvia and I were at the front of the line. Ben opened the door to his vehicle and said, "Right this way."

Sylvia and I climbed into the backseat, and two other guests seated themselves in the middle seats.

"Our first stop is about fifteen minutes from here. We'll put out late morning snacks and hot beverages for you while you scan for whales." He pulled out and headed for the ocean.

I started to ask Sylvia how her stay was going but thought better of it, considering what had happened.

"What made you choose to come to Redwood Heights?" I decided was a safer question.

"The guests," she answered promptly. "I noticed a number of celebrities had stayed here, and the town is known to attract them. It was a chance to be among the rich and famous."

That was why she was here? She was a celebrity chaser?

Sylvia shot me a quick glance. "Thank you for helping yesterday." She fiddled with one of the buttons on her navy wool jacket. "I know you didn't find anybody." She paused. "I saved a long time for this vacation." She looked out the window. "I had time to think about what happened. Maybe I did just stumble."

Oh. This was a different take on the situation.

"I'm an administrative secretary at Preston Insurance Company based in Kansas City. I've dreamed of coming here for ages. It's been everything I'd hoped for." She pulled out her camera and began to show me pictures. She prattled on as she identified a couple of movie stars and a television host. It was going to be a long morning.

Ben began his tour guide spiel, interrupting our conversation. "Excuse me, folks, but I'd like to tell you a little about whale watching as we drive to our first stop. These are gray whales moving north to Canada and Alaska. You'll often see their backs as they surface as well as plumes of spray as they spout. Occasionally, they'll spyhop by jumping straight up or breach by coming out of the water and doing a roll."

The vehicle stopped on a high bluff overlooking the ocean. Ben turned to us. "There's a path along the cliff. I'll give you binoculars. We'll be setting up some food on those tables." He pointed to a picnic area. "Please watch your step and don't go too close to the edge. We'll leave in about an hour to go to another viewing area."

He opened the doors and handed each of us a binoculars case with a long strap. Small clusters of people were at various points along the headland. The guests left to join them. Ben opened the back of the Cadillac, and I spied Helen's baskets.

I reached in to help him unload. "I didn't have a chance to tell you this before, but I work for Resorts International. I'm Kelly Jackson, manager of Redwood Cove Bed-and-Breakfast."

He pulled out a box with thermoses. "Nice to meet you."

I helped him remove the rest of the supplies as the other two vehicles arrived. A stocky man walked over wearing a fleece with RED-WOOD HEIGHTS embroidered on the front.

He thrust his hand in my direction. "I'm Claude Baxter."

"Kelly Jackson," I said, as we shook hands.

"Glad to meet you."

The three guides, Claude, and I set the baskets on the tables.

"Thanks for your help," Ben said. "We won't take the food out until we see a guest headed back in this direction."

"I'll come back and help with the setting up when you're ready." I headed off to try to spot a whale for some whale watching of my own.

As I approached the groups of people, I heard a collective "Ahh . . ." followed by an "Ohh . . ." I pulled my binoculars out and looked at the ocean. Several long, glistening whale backs glided through the water. A large spout sprayed from one of the whales, the iridescent rainbow dissipating in the wind. I tingled with excitement. I'd never seen anything like this before.

One of the whales breached, showing his belly and landing with a gigantic splash on his back. The show continued with occasional intermissions when all we saw was the constant motion of the ocean. Then suddenly we'd see them again. A flip of a gigantic tail would elicit another round of admiration from the watchers.

A group was gathered around a man in the olive green uniform of the California Department of Fish and Game. A class of school kids was off to the side. An arm shot up and waved energetically in my direction. Tommy emerged from the group and stood at its edge.

Five people stood behind the children—figures I knew well. The Silver Sentinels had come to see the show. Ivan and Rudy wore cream-colored cable-knit heavy sweaters, identical except in size, given Rudy's slight frame. Ivan towered over his brother. His thick shaggy hair contrasted with Rudy's neatly trimmed mustache and beard. The brothers' dark wool watch caps were pulled down over their ears. Mary and Gertie wore beanies, red and green respectively, their white hair glistening in the sun. The Professor sported a tweed cap today. I joined them.

The crashing waves and the coastal wind gave Ivan's voice no competition. "We come see whales. See many when out in fishing boat. My *Nadia* docked right now. Can only see from land. When fixed, we all go out together. Yah. Fun."

I was standing next to Rudy, and he smiled and said, "It might be a while before that happens, so we've been enjoying them from the land."

The Professor stepped close and spoke in my ear. "We've heard the warden many times, but we never grow tired of listening to him. It's fascinating what the large mammals can do."

Gertie and Mary approached and commandeered my other ear.

"We've seen two spyhops so far," Mary said.

"And there was a breach a few minutes ago," Gertie added.

I increased the volume of my voice to be heard over the sound of the ocean. "I'm really enjoying watching them. I've never seen anything like it."

I spied a member from our group heading back to the vehicles. "I've got to get back to work."

"We'll see you at the party tonight," Gertie said.

"I'm looking forward to it."

A tall, blond woman from our group turned and headed back toward the vehicles, and I followed. The guides had most of the boxes unpacked. I reached for the last one and unloaded chocolate and raspberry croissants.

The rest of the tour group arrived and helped themselves to the pastries.

Sylvia came over to me. "Kelly, as much as I'm enjoying myself, I'd like to go back to the Heights." Her shoulders drooped. "The bruises from my fall are starting to hurt more."

"Of course. I'll talk to the guides."

Another member of the party, Jerry Gershwin, joined us. Sylvia had told me in the car he was a celebrity chef.

"I'd like to go back as well," he said. "My to-do list is a little too long for me to be gone for a whole day."

"I'll go arrange it."

Sylvia straightened up, eyes sparkling. She'd be going back with a star.

I walked up to Ben. "Two people would like to go back now. How can we make that happen?"

"No problem. We have enough room in the other vehicles for the remaining guests. I'll drive you. Let me know when they're ready."

"Okay. Thanks."

I walked back to Sylvia and Jerry. Sylvia was chatting up Jerry as if they were old acquaintances. There was even some eyelash fluttering going on. She was going to have a lot of stories to tell when she went back to work.

"Ben will take us to Redwood Heights when you want to leave."

They finished their coffees and pastries and told me they were ready to go. I let Claude know what was happening and found Ben, who said he'd be with us in a few minutes.

As we waited, a slight frown creased Jerry's forehead as he tried to smooth out his khaki shirt's fold lines. He wore stiff, unfaded denims, and his hiking boots were out-of-the box clean. Had he left on the price tags like I sometimes did by accident?

Ben arrived. I got in the back and sat in the center of the seat, while Sylvia and Jerry settled in the middle row, each next to a window. Sylvia twittered away happily as she flitted like a bird from one favorite morsel to another, gushing over a number of Jerry's recipes. He stroked his goatee and smiled at her, soaking it up. A good pairing. He reached over and gave Sylvia a little pat on her knee. I thought she was going to swoon. Luckily she had her seat belt tightly fastened, but I was prepared to unbuckle mine and grab her from over the back of the seat if necessary.

I spied the mansion and sighed with relief. A silent, solitary day of inventorying sounded divine after the chatter-filled morning.

"It's been a pleasure," Jerry said. "Please excuse me, but I have work to do."

Why would he buy new clothes, come to a posh place like this, and then work? What was that about?

Sylvia and I entered the mansion.

She paused as we reached the lobby. "I'd like some tea to take up to my room."

I walked with her to the parlor.

A woman in a green velvet Victorian gown stood at the tea service. She looked up as we entered. "Hello. I'm Lily Wilson. I work here at the inn leading tours and helping with a variety of tasks."

"Nice to meet you. I'm Kelly Jackson, manager of Redwood Cove B and B."

Lily turned to Sylvia. "Good morning, Mrs. Porter. May I make you tea or pour you coffee?"

"Tea would be wonderful. Something with lemon." Sylvia pulled out her camera and said to me, "Here's another photo I took yesterday."

She held up the camera, and I saw a handsome man with dark hair and another gentleman in the background.

"Robert Johnson, one of the richest men in the country." She grinned. "And staying here, the same as little old me."

Lily put the tea down next to her, the citrus smell filling the room, and looked at the picture. "You take wonderful photographs, Mrs. Porter."

"Thank you." Sylvia turned to me. "I want to rest a bit and maybe take a nap. I'd appreciate it if you'd come and get me if I'm not down for the house tour at one. I can't figure out the alarm in the room, and my travel clock isn't always reliable."

"I'd be happy to," I replied.

Sylvia left and Lily approached me. "You're welcome to join the tour," she said. "It's for our guests as well as the general public. I have twelve people signed up, which is normally the limit of participants. However, it's not uncommon for me to add one more to accommodate families and groups of friends."

"Thanks. I'll see how the day goes."

I went and let Hensley know I was back. She asked me to meet in the library at twelve thirty to introduce the live-in staff. There were others who came in for the day, but she wanted me to know the main employees. I headed for the storage shed. The termite and bedbug crew drove into the yard. Stevie waved and two beagle heads popped into view. Daniel pulled in behind the motor home in his faded blue van.

"Hi!" I greeted them.

"Hi," Stevie replied as he opened the door and got out. The dogs did a beagle bugle hello, their barks hitting some high notes.

Daniel joined us. "Stevie's finished your place and is ready to do his work here. He'll be staying—"

He didn't get a chance to finish his sentence.

Margaret Hensley burst out of the mansion. "Get that thing out of here now." Her teeth were clenched and her face almost purple.

"But . . . but . . ." Stevie sputtered, rooted to the ground.

"You heard me, now!" She raised her hand and shoved her index finger at his face.

Daniel stepped in front of Stevie, blocking Hensley's gesture. His dark eyes looked down at her. "Michael Corrigan wants Steven here. He has permission to work on site until his job is completed."

"On site? That abomination parked here? With giant termites and bedbugs on the side?"

"But . . . but . . ." Stevie tried to intervene. His eyes blinked rapidly behind his gold-rimmed glasses.

"We'll see about that," she hissed and stormed away.

The woman had a serious temper. What would happen if she really lost it?

Chapter 5

Stevie's face was bright red. "Daniel, you know I'd never leave the sides of the motor home showing. I'm always careful about that. I wouldn't . . ."

"I know and Michael Corrigan knows that as well," Daniel said. "And better yet, Margaret Hensley will know as soon as she speaks with Michael."

The color in Stevie's face began to return to normal.

"Why don't you go park the RV and get set up? Besides, your kids are waiting for you." Daniel pointed to the beagles crammed onto the dashboard of the vehicle, watching them.

"Okay." Stevie moved toward the motor home. "I'll cover the sides first thing, like I always do." He walked away, head hanging down.

Daniel turned to me with a sigh. "I'll be so glad when Josh, the manager for Redwood Heights, returns. He's been on a medical leave of absence."

"She seems so out of character for the type of person Michael hires."

"They go way back. I don't know the particulars. What I do know is, she relates well with the clientele who frequent this place, but not the personnel. Good help is hard to find in a small community like ours, and a number of the employees have come to me to complain. The only reason they're staying on is they love Josh and know he'll be back."

"I'm glad they're coming to you and not just quitting."

"Me too."

"Is there something you can offer them? You know, hazardous duty benefits?"

Daniel laughed. "Not a bad idea. I'll think about it. What are you up to?"

"I'm going to the carriage house to start the inventory."

"I'll see you later. If you need help with anything, let me know."

"Shall do."

We waved good-bye, and I walked up path next to the mansion, following directions for what I'd been told was the quickest way to reach my destination. I rounded a corner and stopped to gaze at the massive white building in front of me. At one time, its oversize doors had allowed grand carriages to pass through. I walked up to it.

A faded coat of arms decorated the front above the doors. On the shield, the silhouettes of two rearing horses faced each other. Crossed rifles were at the top of the crest and tall redwood trees filled in the back of the crest. The words on the banner had faded with time.

Ornate wrought-iron handles graced the doors. I tugged on them, but the doors didn't budge. They were probably bolted from the inside. I spotted a normal-size door off to one side and walked over to it. Even that humble door had a knob that was a work of art.

The skeleton key fit perfectly. I opened the door, flipped the light switch I found next to it, and surveyed the cavernous room. Boxes were piled high to my right and along one wall. Large oak barrels were lined up in stacks at the back of the room. High windows on two sides of the room added some light, but it was dim at best. The brochure I'd read said there'd been a cave turned into a wine cellar. It later became part of the current structure.

I approached the cartons and ran an experimental finger along the top of one. The dust was so thick you could write a legible message in it. I looked around. The only thing not covered in a blanket of dust was the bright red fire extinguisher next to the door. The fire code kept that current.

I took the lid off of one of the boxes and sneezed. And sneezed again and again. Mom used to tease me I sneezed like a truck driver; though I don't know how many of those people she'd heard. Years of motionless dirt sprang to life and dust motes spiraled upward in shafts of sunlight, creating a ballet of particles.

I examined the contents of four boxes. Two contained Christmas ornaments and books. A third one had legal documents dated about fifty years ago and a fourth had old, yellowing newspaper clippings and photos. One photo showed dappled Percherons hitched to a carriage with the same coat of arms I'd seen outside. They towered over the man holding their bridles.

Inventorying these would be challenging, as well as dirty. I looked around. There wasn't any table for me to spread things out on. It'd be much easier back at Redwood Cove B & B, where I could set up a work area in the garage. I decided I'd ask Hensley if I could take them there.

I stepped outside and locked the door. The fresh smell of the redwoods washed away the dust lingering in my lungs. I glanced at my watch. It was time to meet the staff members Hensley had assembled. I was glad they were staying on in spite of the temperamental manager.

I entered the library, where three people waited. One of them was Lily, and she gave me a welcoming wave. She'd added a rakish hat with a large feather to her ensemble.

A moment later, Hensley entered. "Hello, everyone. I want you to meet Kelly Jackson. She's the new manager of Redwood Cove Bed-and-Breakfast. She's been assigned to inventory some items here at the mansion, while renovations are completed." The manager turned to Lily. "This is Lily Wilson."

"We met this morning," I said and smiled at the woman in Victorian garb.

"Lily does many things here at Redwood Heights, as well as being our historian. If you have any questions about the mansion's past, she's the one to talk to."

I looked at Tina Smith, who was one of the group. "Thank you for the brochure. I enjoyed learning about Redwood Heights." I turned to Hensley and said, "Tina and I met yesterday afternoon as I was getting ready to leave."

Hensley nodded and introduced the last person in the room, a pale, thin young woman with short blond hair. "This is Cindy Watson. She and Tina help with housekeeping and preparing food for the guests. They are attending a raw cooking food school."

"Nice to meet you," I said. "I've heard of raw cooking schools, but I don't know much about them."

"Tina and I'd be happy to share what we know. Let's meet for coffee sometime."

"I'd like that," I replied. "It's nice meeting all of you. I look forward to getting to know you."

"Welcome," Lily said.

The others nodded in agreement.

"Thanks." I turned to Hensley. "I opened four boxes in the carriage house. They contained books, Christmas ornaments, newspaper clippings, photos, and what appear to be some old legal documents. I think it'd be a lot easier to inventory them at my place. Is that okay with you?"

"That's fine," Hensley said.

"I need to excuse myself," Lily said. "The tour will be gathering shortly."

"I'll go with you to see if Mrs. Porter's there. As you know, she wants to go on it and was worried about her alarm not working," I said.

"That's an exquisite dress," I commented as Lily and I walked to the lobby area.

"It's a replica of a traveling dress Mrs. Brandon wore in a photograph." Lily stroked the forest green velvet sleeves ending in fine black lace. "A friend of mine made it, paying close attention to detail."

"The beading at the bodice must have taken hours."

"I'm sure it did. I really treasure it. I helped my friend Gladys when she was ill, and this was a thank-you gift."

We entered the registration area. Eight people were already assembled and three more arrived as we walked in. Lily moved to the front of the group of eleven people. I'd been told the maximum size was twelve. Sylvia hadn't joined them yet.

"Welcome, everyone. My name is Lily Wilson, and I'll be leading the tour today. If you have questions, please don't hesitate to ask them. There's a sign-in sheet on the check-in counter."

Several people headed in that direction.

Lily looked at her watch. "We'll be starting at one o'clock, which is in five minutes." She turned in my direction and said, "I'd like to introduce the manager of one of Resorts International properties, Kelly Jackson. She's in charge of Redwood Cove Bed-and-Breakfast."

The members of the group smiled an acknowledgment.

A short man in a denim shirt and khaki pants raised his hand.

Lily smiled at him and asked, "Is there something you'd like to know?"

He pointed to the entrance to the parlor. "What is that shield above the doorway?"

"Redwood Heights was built by Reginald Brandon. That's the family coat of arms," Lily said. "There is an official Brandon crest on file. However, Mr. Brandon wanted to design his own to reflect life in the West. On his shield he chose to put the silhouettes of two rearing stallions, symbols of strength. Rifles instead of swords crossed over the top of them—the weapons of that era. Tall redwood trees filled in the area behind them and were the source of his wealth. You can see his motto for loyalty and honor on the banner."

I enjoyed her explanation. It added another dimension to an object that had just been an interesting piece.

A tall woman with a long brown braid down her back pointed to a picture. "Is this Mr. and Mrs. Brandon?"

"Yes, that picture is of the Brandons," Lily replied. "The woman in the picture is the second Mrs. Brandon. As with many wealthy families and historic estates, there are questionable stories in their past. Redwood Heights is no different."

"How so?" asked the woman.

"We don't have any pictures of the first Mrs. Brandon. She was the belle of glittering New York high society who found herself in remote Redwood Cove. She disappeared not long after arriving. Some say she ran off with a lover. Rumors cropped up that she took a sizeable amount of Brandon's money, changed her name, and left to enjoy San Francisco's growing attractions."

The cadence of Lily's voice took the story beyond a runaway wife. Her tilted head and arched eyebrow led you down a path of mystery and intrigue. The visitors moved a little closer.

Lily leaned toward them and whispered, "Some say she never left at all." Her words lingered in the dead silence.

Everyone was still—frozen in that past time. Goose bumps popped up on my arms. Someone coughed, and the spell was broken.

"After a time, Brandon married again. They had no children and, alas, the house went to a distant cousin."

I'd been mesmerized by the tale. Snapping out of it, I looked around. Sylvia still wasn't there.

"The tour will meet in the parlor. Restrooms are down the hallway to your right," Lily instructed the group.

I walked up the carpeted stairs to the second floor, running my hand over the smooth oak railing. It had taken hundreds of polishings to develop the fine patina and rich glow.

Sylvia's room was the first door at the top of the staircase. I knocked quietly. When there was no response, I knocked harder. *She must really be a sound sleeper.* I tried the door, but it was locked.

I rushed downstairs, retrieved her room key, and glanced at my watch. If Sylvia hurried, she'd still have time to make the start of the tour. Arriving back at her door, I knocked again.

"Mrs. Porter, it's Kelly. The tour is starting in a couple of minutes." I got no response, so I unlocked the door and peeked in. Sylvia was sitting in front of her dressing table, her back to me.

I opened the door a little farther. "Mrs. Porter?" I stepped inside the room. In the filtered light from the curtained windows, Sylvia's image reflected in the mirror. Her eyes were closed, and her head rested on her shoulder. She must have dozed off before making it into bed for a nap.

My attention was drawn to a brooch on the left side of Sylvia's blouse as I approached her. I hadn't noticed it before. It was a lovely piece—a large egg-shaped pearl surrounded by a burst of red.

I touched Sylvia's shoulder. No response.

"Mrs. Porter?" I gently shook her.

Sylvia's head rolled forward and hung down. Her dangling hair covered the side of her face.

I gasped, and my heart began to pound. I looked more closely at her. The burst of red wasn't part of a pin—it was blood.

Chapter 6

My heart beat against the side of my ribs as if trying to escape. Sylvia was dead.

Or was she?

I had to check her pulse. My body began to tremble. I reached for her wrist. Picking up her limp arm pushed me to the edge, but I kept going, and touched her still-warm flesh. No pulse. Then I reached out to her neck, willing myself to be steady. It took all my mental strength to press against her throat with two fingers. Again, no sign of life.

I felt rooted to the ground, unable to move. I looked around. Her room key was on the gold brocade bedspread. Black leather walking shoes sat neatly beside each other, tucked under the still-made bed. Everything so normal, yet so completely not.

My breathing came in short, shallow gasps. I forced myself to breathe deeply and backed away from the image in the mirror, the body in the chair. I reached the entrance to the room, pulled the Do Not Disturb sign off the doorknob, and stepped outside. I closed the door, slipped the note over the knob, and struggled to lock it with shaking hands.

A cheerful voice said, "Hello, Kelly."

Startled, I looked over the railing. Lily and her tour group stood below. She nodded and smiled.

I returned the nod, but there was no way a smile was going to make it to my face.

I went to a small alcove at the end of the landing and called 911. I told them what I'd seen and that I thought the woman was dead. I gave them the information they requested and descended the staircase. As I got to the bottom, a young woman from the tour group approached me.

36 • *Janet Finsilver*

"Hello. My name is Sally Walters. I heard Lily introduce you."

I struggled to keep my voice calm and ordinary, even though thoughts of the nearby dead body belied any normalcy. "That's correct."

"My husband and I are enjoying our vacation and would like to extend it a few days. Unfortunately, our place is sold out because of the Whale Frolic. We haven't been able to find lodging anyplace else. Do you have any space available?"

"We aren't open yet, as the inn's being renovated. I expect we'll be open soon."

Sally dug in her purse and pulled out a card. "We have tonight and tomorrow night booked at our current place. If you're open by the time we have to leave, please call us."

I took her card. "I'll do that."

She left to rejoin the group. I walked down the hallway to Hensley's office, feeling like I was moving in slow motion. The numbness contrasted with the turmoil in my mind.

Her door was open, and I looked in. Hensley was on the phone. She put up one finger, which I took to mean she'd be done in a moment. I remained in the doorway. If I positioned myself correctly, I could see Sylvia's room. I'd put the sign out, but one of the workers might knock and go in anyway, thinking she'd forgotten to take it off.

Hensley called out. "I can talk with you now, Kelly."

I glanced into the room, checked the upstairs landing, and walked quickly to Hensley's desk. Leaning close, I said, "Mrs. Porter . . ." The words stuck in my throat. "Mrs. Porter's dead."

"What!" Hensley stood.

"I called nine-one-one." I glanced at the doorway. "Let's talk by the door. I want to keep a watch on her room so no one enters it."

Hensley followed me. "Tell me what's happened." Hensley's whisper was more of a hiss.

"She asked me to come and get her for the house tour if she wasn't there. She'd had problems with the alarm clock." I stopped, my voice thready.

Hensley went to a sideboard, poured a glass of water from a crystal pitcher, walked back, and handed it to me.

I took a sip and cleared my throat. "She's sitting in a chair. There's a red stain on her blouse. I think it's blood."

Hensley paled. "You mean you don't think her death is due to an accident or natural causes?"

The enormity of what had happened hit me. "No, I don't . . ." I stammered. How could it be?

"Show me." Hensley strode out of the office.

"Wait!"

She spun around. "Why?"

"I don't think we should go in there. The police wouldn't want us to."

"I won't touch anything. I want to see for myself what the situation is."

My stomach churned. I didn't want to go back there. With dragging feet, I followed Hensley to Sylvia's room. Since I'd already opened it, my fingerprints would be on the handle. I didn't want the manager's on it as well, so I unlocked the door for her.

"I don't want to go in," I said.

"Fine," Hensley snapped.

In a minute she returned, her face ashen. She looked at me. "What could've happened?"

I shook my head. "I have no idea." I locked the room.

As we descended the stairs, a siren approached. It halted, and a car door slammed, followed by a knock at the front door.

Hensley opened it. "Hello, Deputy Sheriff Stanton."

I glimpsed the familiar form of the deputy on the threshold.

He saw me and nodded. "Ms. Jackson." He turned back to the manager. "Mrs. Hensley, I'm responding to a nine-one-one call. What's happened?"

"One of our guests is dead. I'll show you." Hensley headed toward Sylvia's room, Stanton behind her, and me following.

When we got to the room, the deputy put on latex gloves, and I handed him the key. Hensley and I waited outside the room, avoiding eye contact.

After a couple of minutes, Deputy Sheriff Stanton returned. "I have some things I need to do here. I'd like to meet you both in the office when I'm finished."

"Certainly," replied the manager. "We'll wait for you there."

We made our way back. She sat behind her desk with an uncharacteristic plop. I sagged into one of the chairs across from her. Images of Sylvia's body kept flashing through my mind. What had caused her death? Had someone killed her? I slammed a mental door on that thought. I didn't want to let it in.

After a moment, Hensley straightened. "There's a lot to be done. I need to call Michael Corrigan. Sylvia had some personal items placed in the safe. I'd like you to get those out, as well as look up her registration information. You'll find it in the file cabinet over there." She pointed to an antique oak two-drawer file. "I'm sure Deputy Stanton will want them."

I nodded, relieved to have something to do. Hensley called Corrigan, and I tuned out their conversation, concentrating on the safe's combination. I found one of the red leather pouches guests used to store their valuables with Sylvia's name on it and placed it on Hensley's desk as she continued to fill in our boss on what happened. I located Sylvia's file and put it with the pouch.

Hensley hung up the phone. "Michael and another staff member will be here late tonight."

While I looked forward to seeing Corrigan again, it certainly wasn't under circumstances like this.

"Have you had lunch?"

Lunch? Was she kidding? Even thinking about food made me queasy.

She answered my look. "It's going to be a long afternoon. Doing it on an empty stomach is foolish." She picked up the phone and called the kitchen, ordering sandwiches and coffee. "Other officers will be arriving, I'm sure, and will probably benefit from having food available as well."

Deputy Sheriff Stanton knocked on the frame of the open door then entered. "I'm going to need to ask you both some questions about Mrs. Porter."

"Of course, Deputy Stanton. Here are the personal items she had in our safe, along with her registration and emergency contact information." She pushed them across her desk.

"Thank you. I'll look at those later." His gaze took us both in. "I'm considering this a possible homicide. Please don't give out any information to anyone who isn't one of the investigators."

Possible homicide. Murder. The words have been spoken. It is real. My breathing started to speed up again.

"I understand, Deputy Stanton," Hensley said.

I couldn't believe she didn't even bat an eye at the word *homicide*.

"I'm sure you and the others have a lot to do," she added. "I've ordered sandwiches and coffee. Please let your people know they're available."

"Appreciate it," the deputy said. "I've called San Martin police headquarters for assistance. They're sending two detectives. They'll have questions of their own. Now, who found the body?"

"I did," I replied.

"Has anyone else been in the room since the body was found?" Deputy Stanton asked.

"I believe I'm the only one," Hensley said. "Kelly unlocked the door for me but didn't go in again."

"Who has keys to the room?" Deputy Stanton asked.

Hensley went to the cabinet behind her. "There are three keys for every room. The guest has one, one's on the master board, and a third one on the key ring." She pulled out the round wire holding the room keys and located the one to Sylvia's room.

I chimed in. "Deputy Stanton, I gave you the one I used. It's the master board key. I saw Sylvia's key on her bed."

He pulled the metal skeleton key from his pocket. "A duplicate could be made, but it wouldn't be easy, and it'd take time." He looked at the manager. "How long had Mrs. Porter been here?"

"Two days," she replied.

"Did she request a specific room before she arrived?"

Hensley pulled Sylvia's file toward her. "Not to my knowledge. I'll check her records and ask the registration staff."

He turned to me and opened his notepad. "What time did you discover the body?"

"Shortly before one o'clock."

"When did you last see Mrs. Porter alive?"

"A little before eleven thirty when she left with her tea."

"Tell me what you saw when you entered the room."

I told him about going there at Sylvia's request, having to get a key when she didn't respond, and what I saw as I entered the room.

"I thought she'd fallen asleep. I went to wake her, and that's when I noticed what I thought was a brooch on her shoulder."

"Why would you think that?"

"The room was dim because she'd lowered the shades. I saw what I thought was a dark red flower with a pearl in the center."

He frowned at me. "Describe the pearl."

"It was egg-shaped and was in the center of . . . what I now know is blood."

He snapped his book closed. "Come with me." The deputy inclined his head in the direction of the hallway.

No, not again. I didn't want more images of her lifeless body. Once again, I took the long walk to Sylvia's room.

When we got there, Stanton opened the door and gestured me in. My feet felt like they were blocks of lead. Sylvia's body seemed to have slouched more into the chair.

"You said you saw a pearl. Where?"

I looked at the image in the mirror. There was no pearl. I stepped closer and peered at Sylvia's shoulder. There was the red burst of blood but nothing else.

"It was there, a large, egg-shaped pearl . . ." I talked faster. "I'm positive. I saw it. I thought it was a piece of jewelry."

"Slow down, Ms. Jackson," Stanton said. "Tell me about what happened after you left the room."

"I locked the door, called nine-one-one, and went to Mrs. Hensley. We came back because she wanted to see the situation for herself. When she came out, I locked the room again, and as we went downstairs, we heard you arrive. You were the next person in the room."

"Let's talk with Mrs. Hensley."

The deputy and I didn't speak as we returned to the office.

Deputy Sheriff Stanton stood in front of the manager's desk. "Mrs. Hensley, I'd like you to describe what you saw on Mrs. Porter's shoulder where the injury is."

"A bloodstained area appearing to be about five inches in diameter," she replied. "I have no idea what caused it."

"You saw nothing resembling a pearl?"

"A pearl?" The manager shook her head. "No. I didn't see anything but blood."

My head began to spin. The staircase was visible from the hallway leading to the office. There wasn't time for someone to go up it and get in and out of the room in the short time I'd stepped into the office and spoken with Hensley. The manager had gone in by herself. Had she taken the pearl? If so, why? Was it part of what had killed Sylvia? Was Margaret Hensley somehow connected to what had happened?

Chapter 7

Deputy Sheriff Stanton's phone rang. He listened for a moment. "Got it. I'll meet you at the door."

A white van drove by the window . . . the coroner's van. I shuddered, thinking of the body upstairs.

Stanton said, "I'd like you both to stay here until I get back. I want to find out about Mrs. Porter's interactions with you and others as soon as possible."

Hensley and I nodded, and the deputy left.

The Heights manager held out a paper. "Kelly, I was going to ask you to do this when I wasn't in the office. However, since you have to stay, this seems like it would be a good time for you to do this."

I walked over and took the paper. It was another inventory list like the ones I'd gotten earlier.

Hensley pointed to a glass cabinet in the corner of the office. "You'll find the items over there. It's unlocked."

I was more than happy to have something to take my mind off of what had happened. Opening the cabinet, I took out a silver snuffbox. An engraved silhouette of a horse, a barn, and several trees decorated the top. I found it on the list and took a picture. I shot a quick look at the manager behind her desk.

She was the only one I'd seen enter the room after me—and the pearl was there when I left. If she had taken the pearl, where had she put it? She wore a knee-length straight black skirt with a matching fitted cropped jacket. I didn't see any pockets. Could she have held it against her side underneath her top without my noticing?

Hensley wasn't watching me. The box was similar in size to the pearl, and I pinned it against my body with my arm. My arm took on an awkward, unnatural look. Even as upset as I was, I think I would've noticed the odd angle.

Could she have tucked it into the waistband of her skirt? She'd be taking a real chance on it falling out. I doubted she'd do that. Did she know some secret hiding place in Sylvia's room? Had she taken the pearl and hidden it there? Was there a time when I wasn't looking at her after we left the room?

I took another item from the cabinet and tried to remember if I'd turned my back on her as we walked back to the office. I might've done that as she came out of the room. But where would she have hidden it on the landing? After the first few steps, we'd walked side by side. I'd go back and search at the first opportunity. Deputy Stanton didn't believe it existed so wouldn't be looking for it.

But he would be trying to find a murder weapon. Murder. Hard to believe. And it had happened so close to us. How could a stranger have come in unnoticed? Unless it wasn't a stranger. It could be a guest or staff member.

I swallowed hard and glanced at Hensley again. She was alone when I had come to get her . . . and she had access to the room key. I'd seen her temper and knew she didn't like Sylvia Porter, but murder? It didn't seem likely.

Sylvia had annoyed the staff and probably some of the guests, but that didn't seem a strong enough motive for murder, either. I shook my head and gave up trying to figure it out. I didn't know enough about Sylvia or what had happened before I arrived.

Yesterday's fall. Had that been attempted murder or an accidental trip? If someone had tried to kill her, would the outcome today have been different if we'd believed her? A knot formed in my stomach. Had we unwittingly helped her murderer?

Tina appeared in the doorway, pushing a cart. Clearly she was feeling better. She had a tray of quartered sandwiches, thermoses, cups, and the usual accompaniments.

"Please put those over there." Hensley pointed to an oak table at the back of the room.

Tina arranged the food and beverages. "Is there anything else you need, Mrs. Hensley?"

"Not right now."

As Tina went out, the deputy came back in and shut the door behind him. "Kelly, I'd like to talk to you about Mrs. Porter, since you were with her today. Tell me what took place."

I went over the morning's events.

"Did she seem upset?"

"No, she actually said she'd probably just tripped yesterday. I took it as an apology of sorts."

"Anything else you can think of?"

"Not really. Sylvia seemed excited about being here. She was an administrative secretary for Preston Insurance Company in Kansas City, and she'd saved a long time for this trip."

"Thanks. You don't need to stay any longer, but I'll need you to be available when the detectives arrive."

"Okay." I turned to Hensley. "I'll work on the parlor inventory."

"Good idea."

A knock on the door interrupted us.

"Come in," Hensley said.

Daniel walked in. "Hello, Deputy Sheriff Stanton, Mrs. Hensley." He nodded at me.

Stanton nodded and touched the brim of his hat.

Daniel turned toward the desk and said, "Mrs. Hensley, I saw the coroner's van. I wondered if there was anything I could do to help."

"Thank you, Daniel. Give me a minute. I haven't had time to determine what we need to do next."

"Daniel," Deputy Stanton said, "there's been an incident with one of the guests. A Sylvia Porter. Did you have any interaction with her? Or see her with anyone?"

"No. I knew who she was, but what I've been doing hasn't involved the guests. I don't come in the house much. My work's been mostly outside."

"Thanks. If you remember anything or hear something, let me know."

"Sure thing."

Hensley looked at her watch. "Daniel, Lily's tour ended a couple of minutes ago. The visitors parked at the back of the house. I'd like you to go there and be sure no one comes back in to look around. It isn't part of the event, but we've had it happen before."

"Happy to."

I picked up my camera and the paperwork. "I'll come with you."

"What happened?" Daniel asked as we walked down the carpeted hallway.

"Sorry. I wish I could tell you, but I can't. I promise I'll fill you in as soon as I can."

"I understand."

"I thought you were working at your inn this afternoon. How did you find out something had happened?"

Daniel looked a little sheepish and gave me a lopsided grin. "You can thank the Silver Sentinels. Rudy was on his way to chess club, and Deputy Stanton's car went flying by, sirens and lights going. It turned down the hill, and he wondered if it was headed to Redwood Heights."

Daniel paused.

"And then . . ." I prompted.

"He called Gertie, and she called Stevie and . . ."

I laughed. "I get the drift."

"Then when Mary saw the coroner's van go by, she called Gertie . . ."

"I can see where this story goes, and I can finish it. The phone lines must've been sizzling. I hope they didn't melt."

"I wouldn't be surprised if they did."

We reached the back porch. The visitors were beginning to drive away. Two couples chatted with each other. Their laughter floated up to us. I settled in an Adirondack chair, gazed at the towering redwoods, and breathed in their fresh scent.

Daniel leaned on the porch railing. "Are you going to Stevie's birthday party tonight?"

"Yes, unless I have to be here for some reason."

"Stevie's a great guy. A real salt-of-the earth type."

"He has one of the softest voices I've ever heard."

"Matches his personality. Gentle. Quiet. Compassionate. He rescued Jack and Jill. When he got them, they had some serious issues. He had the patience of a saint with them."

"They're sure a happy pair now."

A car door slammed. We looked at the lot. A car drove out and the last couple got in their vehicle and left.

Daniel turned to me. "I'll go see if there's anything else I can do."

"I'm off to inventory the parlor."

Walking through the kitchen, I decided a cup of coffee would help the afternoon speed along. After pouring some from the pot on the coffee warmer, I took a sip, hoping the taste matched the invigorating aroma. It did. Resorts International served blue ribbon coffee, in my opinion.

I entered the parlor and put my camera and inventory sheets on a table near the display case. A routine task with a murdered woman upstairs. It seemed surreal. The ticking clock on the mantel sounded louder. I hadn't noticed it before. Now it destroyed the silence in the room. I picked up the list and forced myself to concentrate.

These items had been photographed in groups and there were notes made below each picture. I planned to take individual photographs and label each one. A backdrop for the pieces would be nice. In the credenza, I found a stack of starched white linen napkins, removed a couple, and spread them on the table.

I took the small shiny metal key from my pocket and unlocked the cabinet. This one held jewelry, beaded evening purses, and a number of items I couldn't identify. My ex-husband would've known what they were. Ken, a university history professor, would be in seventh heaven telling me about each item and what purpose it served.

I pulled out twelve well-crafted silver spoons with intricate designs. From museum trips with Ken, I knew they were apostle spoons. They were used as christening presents, and the spoon represented the baby's apostle.

I had learned about them on our European honeymoon. Ken's passion for history flowed through his voice as we viewed the different exhibits. And I remembered his passion for me.

I sighed, photographed the spoons, and put them back. I pulled out another piece of silver. It seemed to resemble a fish, with fins on one side and a split tail. I had no idea what it was. Betsy, once my best friend, would have recognized it. While I thought history was interesting, Betsy and Ken lived for it. Now they lived for each other.

My mind drifted back to how it all started. Betsy and I had met at a local stable where I volunteered to exercise horses a couple of times a week. Betsy boarded her mare there, and we became riding buddies. I discovered she taught high school history and invited her over for dinner, thinking Ken might be able to give her some ideas for her classes. She ended up getting a lot more than some lesson plans.

I shook my head. *Get over it. It's time to forget and move on.*

I reviewed my list, decided it was the knitting sheath, and checked it off. A note said it held knitting needles and explained how it was used. A needle was put in it, allowing the woman's right hand to be free to handle the yarn. It helped her to work more quickly and efficiently, especially when walking. I remembered from my history classes it was a hard time for many people, and every minute was precious in terms of what it took to keep a roof over their heads and food on the table, even knitting while walking.

Retrieving a glittering evening bag, I marveled over the detailed beaded pattern. I ran my fingers over its surface and then opened it. Was it my imagination, or did I detect a scent of lavender?

Next, I pulled out a blue velvet cushion full of hatpins, their jeweled array creating a sparkling bouquet of colors and shapes. I smiled as I remembered seeing a display and reading about how young women had used them to protect themselves against unwanted advances such as in a public carriage when a stranger's hand moved where it shouldn't.

My camera's battery light blinked, indicating it was low. I'd have to finish this tomorrow. I put the things away and locked the case. Maybe there would be a chance for me to check the landing. I headed for the reception area. Bad timing. They were bringing Sylvia's body down. I averted my eyes and walked to the office.

I knocked and heard Hensley say, "Enter."

The deputy sheriff sat across from her at the desk, an open notepad in front of him.

"Deputy Stanton, I need to recharge my camera battery. Would it be okay for me to go back to my place and work on the boxes from the carriage house?"

Before he could answer, his phone rang. "I see . . . interesting . . . thanks." He looked at Hensley, then me. "Sylvia Porter's emergency contact information led us to a disconnected phone."

I wondered what had happened. As an administrative secretary, Sylvia had to be good with details. I found it hard to believe she'd made a mistake.

Stanton continued. "I gave them the name of the company she told you she worked for. They have no record of a Sylvia Porter."

I knew I had the company name right. Preston was my mother's maiden name, and I'd fleetingly wondered if there was a connection somewhere in the family tree.

"What that means is"—Deputy Stanton leaned back—"we don't have any idea who the dead woman is."

Chapter 8

"We'll find out," Deputy Stanton added. "It'll just take some time."

Sylvia not who she said she was? Why had she lied? "Did she have identification in her purse?" I asked.

"No purse."

"She had one with her on the whale watching trip," I said.

"Thanks for letting me know," Deputy Stanton said. "Working at your place is fine as long as the detectives can reach you when they get here."

"You have my cell phone number and the inn's number."

"Right," he said.

I stepped outside and filled my lungs with the scent of redwoods and tangy ocean air. The light mist carried by the breeze cooled my face and slowed my racing thoughts. The soft melody of the rustling leaves soothed my raw nerves. The short walk back to my inn didn't give me answers, but it helped clear the cobwebs in my mind. I got in my Jeep and headed to the carriage house. On the way, I passed Stevie and his bouncing pair of beagles. They were harnessed and looked ready to work. We exchanged waves. As I went by the four-car garage, I saw part of the side of his RV peeking out from behind it; the sign advertising the beagles and their trade was covered as promised.

I parked and grabbed the faded denim shirt I stored on the backseat for whatever need might arise. The last time it had encased a terrified poodle ready to make my hand into a sausage. I'd stopped traffic in both directions on a busy road when I saw him running between cars. The same dog melted into his grateful owner's arms, then smiled at me and licked my hand when I'd reached to retrieve my shirt.

After slipping it on, I loaded the dust-covered boxes and drove back to the B & B. The work shed housed a large wooden table, convenient for a variety of projects. I put the boxes on it, sneezing as the dust found new life from the action. I'd unpacked two of my moving cartons the night before and decided I'd go into the house to get them in order to transfer some of these things into clean containers.

The kitchen held the sweet lingering fragrance of the morning's baking. A warm, embracing smell, it helped to push out some of the cold memories of the afternoon. A plastic-wrapped plate sat on the counter. A croissant laced with miniature chocolate chips called my name, and I ignored it . . . at first. Then I gave in and savored the rich butteriness and the hint of chocolate. This was my new life. How lucky could one get? I allowed myself a sigh of pleasure and continued on to my living quarters.

I returned to the shed and got to work. Legal documents went into one box. I planned to examine them in my room. In the other, I placed the pictures and newspaper articles, glancing at them as I did so. There was some fascinating history in those yellowed papers. The Silver Sentinels might have fun sorting through them. I called the Professor.

"Hello, my dear. So wonderful to hear your voice and have you back with us."

"I'm glad to be here, too."

"I'm sorry to hear there seems to have been foul play at the Heights. Not a fun start to your return."

Startled, I asked, "What do you know about it?"

"It's a simple equation. The coroner's van and the deputy sheriff's car go by. People are being questioned. You can't talk about it. In all probability, it's murder."

"But . . . how . . ."

"You sound a bit surprised. I called Daniel to find out what he knew. As you know, we all take part when something is afoot, and that was my assignment."

The sleuthing Silver Sentinels are on it again.

"I'll bring you up to speed when I can," I said.

"We know you will."

"I called because I have a project the group might be interested in." I explained what I found.

"Delightful idea. I'll call the others and get back to you."

I turned my attention to the box full of Christmas ornaments. Placing them on the table, I didn't think they looked special. Probably common ones used around the house. After photographing them in batches, I packed them in the carriage house box I'd emptied. The books in the last carton didn't appear rare. Nothing jumped out at me from the titles, authors, or copyright dates. I lined them up six at a time and photographed their spines and put them back in their box. An Internet search would tell me if they were valuable.

I looked around for something to label them with, but no luck. I'd take care of that tomorrow.

I put the ornaments and books back in my Jeep. As I started to pick up the box of legal papers to take to the inn, my phone rang.

"The group's excited about seeing what you've unearthed," the Professor said.

"Great. I'll get the conference room ready for you for tomorrow morning."

"Perfect. We're looking forward to it."

I transferred the clippings and photos into the other clean box and carried it to the meeting room. It would be fun to have them here, and work with them again. I retrieved the last box and headed back inside the inn. Helen stood at the kitchen counter.

Fred was stretched out in a rectangle of sun and beat a tune with his tail in greeting.

"Hi," she said. "Are you going to be able to make the party tonight?"

I put the box on the counter. "I think so."

"I'll leave directions for you."

"Thanks."

Helen opened the refrigerator, and I noticed a cake. But this wasn't just any cake. Bright spirals of color—orange, red, green, purple, and blue—swirled around the sides and top. It was the first psychedelic-looking frosting I'd ever seen. It matched Stevie's tie-dyed top.

She pulled it out and put it on the counter.

"Wow! That looks amazing."

A little pink colored her face. "Thanks. I made it for Stevie's party. I still have some decorating to do."

"It's a real work of art."

The conversation halted as Tommy burst into the room. "Hi, Mom, Miss Kelly."

But he wasn't looking at us. He only had eyes for the dancing hound in front of him.

Fred began baying, and Tommy chimed in, howling along with him.

"Good grief! Enough, you two." Helen said. She looked at me. "Are you sure you're ready for this?"

I laughed. "Absolutely!"

Tommy got a bottle of juice from the refrigerator and sat at the counter.

"I've started a side business doing custom baking," Helen said. "It's been fun. I love to cook, and I'm beginning to get to know some of the locals."

Tommy managed to bounce up and down on the flat wooden stool. "I'm the official taste tester."

"I look forward to hearing more about it. See you two later."

I picked up the carton and went back to my room. Putting it next to the couch for later, I stretched and thought about another cup of coffee. My phone rang, and I recognized Hensley's number.

"Kelly, Deputy Stanton would like you to come back. The detectives are here, and he has more questions for you."

"I'm on my way."

I paused in the kitchen. Helen was bending over the cake and writing on the top with a piping bag, like my mom used. The name *Stevie* appeared in bright turquoise letters.

"I have to go the Heights. Unless something unusual happens, I should still be able to make the party at some point. I might be late."

"Okay. I'll let the others know."

"Thanks," I said.

"Oh, Phil and Andy checked in yesterday."

Sommelier Phil—short for Philopoimen—Xanthis provided the wine for the inn. He and cheese monger Andy Brown created pairings for the guests. They were supplying Redwood Heights the cheese and wine for the Whale Frolic festival. I'd told them they could stay at Redwood Cove B & B, even though we weren't officially open for guests. There were still a few minor details that needed to be taken care of, but the rooms were ready.

I opened the Jeep's door, took off my denim shirt, and tucked it away for its next adventure. Daniel's VW bus was ahead of me as I drove down the road to the mansion. We parked next to each other and walked in together.

"Have you heard anything new?" I asked him.

"Nope. Hensley didn't have anything else for me to do, so I left." We went to the office in silence, where we found Hensley and Stanton seated at the desk.

Deputy Sheriff Stanton ran a roughened hand over his face. "I appreciate your promptness. Do either of you have anything to add to what you've already told me about the woman called Sylvia Porter?"

We both shook our heads. Neither of us had had much to do with Sylvia . . . or whoever she was.

"We're trying to figure out what besides her purse might be missing. Did you see her carrying anything?"

"She had a camera," I said.

"Did you notice what kind?

"No, sorry."

"I have a list of the jewelry she had on," he said. "I'd like the three of you to look at it."

Hensley spoke up after perusing the items. "She had an unusual pendant that isn't listed here. Belonged to her mother."

"I'll get a description of it later from you." Stanton jotted in his notepad. "You've had some jewelry thefts here. Refresh my memory."

"The last couple of days a few items have gone missing. I'm still reluctant to call it robbery. I'm hoping it's a coincidence two guests misplaced their things. However, the jewelry's gone, and I needed to report it. Both incidents happened during afternoon tea. The guests left their rooms unlocked when they went to the parlor."

Has the thief upped the ante?

"I understand all the current guests were staying here at the same time as the murdered woman," Stanton said.

"That's correct."

"Do you know what any of them were doing between eleven thirty and twelve forty-five?"

"Yes, as a matter of fact I do. Twelve people went on a whale-watching trip and then had a catered lunch accompanied by Claude Baxter, a chef who works with us part-time, and a wine steward he knows. They explained the special attributes of the meal. The others were on an all-day horseback riding excursion we arranged."

"So they all have alibis, sounds like," Stanton said.

"Except for Jerry Gershwin," I volunteered. "He came back with Sylvia."

"Is there anyone else who stayed here and has left who might have had contact with her?"

"The only person would be a Robert James," Hensley replied.

"I'd like to see his registration and payment information."

Hensley pulled a paper from a manila folder on her desk. "I can show you what he put down, but there's no payment record. He paid cash."

"That seems unusual," I blurted out. *Oops. No one asked for my opinion.*

Hensley handed the form to the deputy. "Identity theft has caused more people to do cash transactions. I didn't think anything of it."

"Can you tell me anything about him?" Deputy Stanton asked.

"He was a walk-in. We'd had a last-minute cancellation, so it worked out. He only stayed one night. Checked out yesterday."

Daniel volunteered, "I ran into him while I was working outside. He asked me about some of the outlying buildings. Wanted to know their history."

Stanton nodded. "We'll see what we can learn about him, though there's nothing to indicate finding him is a priority."

Daniel spoke up. "He's still in town. At least he was as of lunchtime today. We were celebrating my daughter's good grades with a pizza, and I saw him."

Hensley's brow creased. "I wonder why he checked out, since the room was still available."

Daniel shrugged. "He was with some guy I didn't recognize."

"Thanks." Stanton turned to Hensley. "What about your staff during that time?"

"All the live-in staff was present or on errands: They are Cindy Watson, Lily Wilson, and Tina Smith. I don't know if any of them have alibis," Hensley said. "I asked Cindy to bring fresh coffee. She should be here any minute. You can find out what she was doing."

As if on cue, there was a knock on the door.

"Come in," Hensley said.

Cindy opened the door and wheeled in a cart with thermoses on it. She pushed it over to where coffee had been placed earlier and began exchanging containers.

"Ms. Watson, where were you today between eleven thirty and twelve forty-five?"

Cindy stopped what she was doing and faced the deputy. "I went into the parlor and saw Mr. Gershwin working on the computer. He introduced himself, and we talked a bit. I mentioned I was going to the market. He wanted to come along and see what was available and mentioned he'd been working on some new recipes."

"When did you last see him?"

"It was about twenty after twelve. I had to come back here for a meeting. He said he was going to look at restaurant menus. I looked over my shoulder on my way here, and I could see him going up the hill in the opposite direction."

Even if he rushed back after Cindy arrived at the meeting, it's unlikely he'd made it before twelve forty. He didn't seem a likely suspect.

Deputy Stanton turned to me. "The detectives are in the dining room and would like to ask you some questions."

I found them, and we shared introductions. The detectives asked almost the same questions as Deputy Sheriff Stanton. It didn't take long, and I was soon on my way home.

Home. There was that word again. I really liked the sound of it.

I pulled in and saw a gold van parked in the guest lot. Andy and Phil had arrived. I entered the kitchen just as they made a toast.

"To great wine," said Phil. His short tight curls of gray hair covered his head like a cap.

"Paired with phenomenal cheese!" Andy chimed in, and they clinked their glasses together.

"Ah . . . Kelly, so good to see you again." Phil rose and gave me a quick hug. He was about my height, which put him at five feet six inches. "And you're running the inn now. Congratulations!"

"Thanks, Phil. I'm looking forward to settling in here."

Andy gave me a hug as well. "You're just in time to enjoy some luscious flavors!" He waved to a plate with several different cheeses— a blue-veined wedge, a rich orange rectangle, and a creamy round.

Sampling cheese for a living created some diet challenges, and it didn't appear Andy had made much progress on the diet his doctor had ordered. He ran his fingers through his thin light brown hair.

Phil had taught me what a flight of wines was and Andy introduced me to the world of artisan cheese.

"I'll have to pass. I'm off to a birthday party."

"Another time, then," Andy said. The men sat and resumed their sipping and tasting.

Entering my suite, I headed for one of my packed boxes from the ranch. I rooted around in it for a few minutes and found what I was looking for—Mom's homemade huckleberry jam. I pulled two jars out. One would make a nice hostess gift, the other one I'd give to Stevie when I saw him after the party, since Gertie had said, "No gifts please."

I thought back to how much fun we'd had as kids going out to pick the berries. It was a family ritual. My two brothers alternated between pounding on each other and carefully picking the fragile fruit. My sister and I chattered away, filling our buckets and basking in the warm sun of the short Wyoming summer. Grandpa filled us in on how Native Americans used the berries for medicinal purposes.

Grabbing a cobalt blue sweater, I changed out of my fleece and traded jeans for black slacks. Leather walking shoes replaced lightweight hiking boots. Slipping into my down jacket, I was ready to go.

Voices drifted from the parlor, where Andy and Phil had moved. Helen's directions to the party were on the counter. I grabbed them and headed out. In five minutes, I was parking.

When I got to the door, I noticed in the entryway a large patch of red chard. The scarlet veins formed an intricate, vivid pattern on the bright green bumpy surface of the leaves. Something had trampled a large section of the brilliantly colored plants, leaving crushed leaves and jagged red edges on the broken stems. I knocked.

Ivan opened the door. He looked over me, a fierce frown on his face, and stared out at the pitch black night like a warrior ready to battle an unseen enemy. He pushed the door a bit wider. "Come in," he growled, his deep voice rumbling like thunder. "Come. Gertie hurt. She attacked."

Chapter 9

Ivan stepped aside, firmly closed the door behind me, and locked it. I could see people over at a kitchen counter. Mary handed a brown bottle and cotton balls to Helen, who took them and poured some of the liquid from the bottle onto a piece of cotton.

Gertie looked over her shoulder. "Hi, Kelly. Glad you could make it."

The others waved a greeting, but frowns were on their faces. The living room on my left was filled with two beagles, a basset hound, and Tommy rolling around on the floor in front of a wood-burning stove, flames flickering in its window. Divine mouthwatering aromas filled the house. I joined the group gathered around Gertie.

"This is going to sting," Helen said.

"You have no idea how many times I said that to Stevie when he was growing up."

Helen gently dabbed the back of Gertie's hand. A froth of white bubbles appeared. She dried it and applied some antibiotic ointment.

Mary hovered nearby. "How do you feel? Do you need to see a doctor?"

"Heavens, no. They're only superficial scratches. I feel fine."

I leaned over to look at her hand. "What happened?" Angry red lines covered her pale, almost translucent skin.

"Someone tried to take my purse."

"Have you called the police?" I asked.

"No, the person is long gone by now. Probably someone after the new phone Stevie gave me. I was at the deli getting more milk for Tommy and Allie. Alex, the man behind the counter, saw the phone when I went to pay him and commented on it. There were young men hanging around nearby. I wouldn't be surprised if it was one of them."

The Professor cleared his throat. "Even so, I feel you should report it, my dear."

"I will. But there's no reason for the police to waste their time to come out just for this. Billy said he'd stop by later, and I can tell him then."

"Who's Billy?" I asked.

"Deputy Sheriff Bill Stanton. Also known as William when he was misbehaving in my fifth grade class. He said he'd come by for a few minutes."

I repressed a grin. Deputy Sheriff Stanton, the big, serious officer. Billy.

Rudy spoke up. "He'll want a detailed description of the incident and what the person looked like. Do you have some paper I can use? We can get that out of the way now."

Gertie nodded. "Good idea. Then we can get the party started and not have to be interrupted by that later. There's a notepad on the end of the counter."

Rudy retrieved it, along with a pen. He looked quite dapper in a tweed jacket instead of his usual wool sweater. "Okay. What can you tell us?"

"I heard a noise behind me as I was about to get out my keys. I felt a sharp pain on my hand and a tug on my purse. I turned away, and my purse slid off my shoulder into the corner of the entryway. The person lunged for it."

Gertie gave a triumphant smile and held up her metal cane. "Then I gave the attacker what for with this. I whacked whoever it was on the arm twice and once on the head. I heard a grunt, too."

Stevie rested his hand on his mother's shoulder. "I arrived, saw the person lunge, and yelled at them to stop. The person turned and ran."

"That's when I took one more swing, lost my balance, and crushed my poor plants."

Now I know who trampled the chard.

"Male or female?" Rudy asked.

"I don't know. Whoever it was had a knit cap pulled down to the top of their eyes and over their ears. A scarf had been tied over the lower part of the face. They kept their head down when they made their grab."

"Did you get a look at any of the attacker's face?" the Professor asked.

"Just the eyes and nose, but the porch light was too dim to get any details."

Rudy made notes. "What did the person look like overall?"

"I can't tell you much there." Gertie paused and thought for a minute, then looked at me. "The person was about Kelly's height, maybe a little taller."

I am five foot six, so that didn't give us a lot to go on.

"Hard to tell about size. They seemed large, but I don't know if that was because of clothing or body shape."

"Is there anything you can add?" Rudy asked Stevie.

"I saw a glimpse of a dark, puffy coat and sweatpants, but that's it."

Rudy pulled the page he'd written from the notepad. "That's done. We'll give it to the deputy sheriff."

Helen started to place a bandage on Gertie's hand.

"Helen, please, wait a minute, and I'll take photographs." I pulled my camera from its case and took a couple of pictures. Maybe they wouldn't have to remove the covering from her fragile skin to see the injury.

Helen applied two large bandages and removed the cuts from sight.

"Now," Gertie said, "let's get this party going. We're here to celebrate my son's birthday!"

"Are you sure you still want to do this?" Mary asked.

"Mary, I'm fine." Gertie got up and gave her friend a hug. "Thanks for your concern. You know me. I never say something I don't mean. If I didn't feel up to it, I'd tell you."

The anxious look left Mary's face. "Yes, Gertie, you always tell it like it is. One of the things I love about you."

The two longtime friends hugged again.

The tension in the room dissipated as smiles replaced frowns, and people began to move around.

Gertie turned to me. "Kelly, you can put your things in the first room on the left." She pointed to a hallway.

"This is for you." I handed her the huckleberry jam. "My mom made it. I brought it from home."

"How sweet of you! I'll try it tomorrow morning."

I left to put my jacket and camera away. Entering the room indicated by Gertie, I was immediately struck by the beautiful quilt covering the bed. A huge multicolored star covered the top, and designs of bird, hearts, and tulips adorned the corners. I'd have to ask Gertie about it. I went back to the main living area.

A knock at the door heralded the arrival of Daniel and Allie.

"I'm glad you two are here. Perfect timing. We're about to start," Gertie said.

Daniel leaned down and gave her a hug. "We've been looking forward to it."

Gertie directed them to the room where I'd put my things. When they returned, she asked us all to gather near the counter.

"I'm very thankful for my wonderful son, Stevie. To celebrate his day of birth, I decided to make his favorite meal, Thanksgiving dinner, and share it with the wonderful friends I'm so grateful to have."

Stevie wrapped his arm around his mom's shoulders, a gentle giant next to a little elf. "Thanks, Mom. That's the best present ever."

We all took turns wishing him a happy birthday, some with hugs, others with a pat on the back.

"While the table is being prepared, would someone go out and get the broken chard for me? I don't want it to go to waste." Gertie held up a woven basket.

"I'd be happy to do it," I said. Besides, I could look around the area and see if the attacker had left anything behind.

"I go, too," Ivan said.

Gertie pulled a large flashlight from its wall mount and handed it to Ivan. She gave me a smaller one from a drawer. She put two pairs of clippers in a basket. Ivan took it outside.

I went to get my coat. As I walked back through the room, helpful hands busied themselves, and dishes flowed out of the refrigerator and oven and off the countertops. Stevie carved the turkey as Gertie directed where to put the food on the table.

I found Ivan glowering into the dark under the porch light. I flicked on the flashlight and began to cut the chard. He'd placed himself with his back to the house and often looked up, seeking anything that might be lurking in the blackness. His silver mane of hair in the porch light reminded me of an Irish wolfhound, his watchfulness that of one protecting its territory.

While I cut, I searched the area, shining my flashlight beam all around. I checked under the broken leaves and beyond, into the uninjured plants. The person had used something to hurt Gertie. She said she hit the attacker on the arm twice. Maybe they'd dropped the weapon.

I stood, stretched, and went over to the doorway. Nothing there. There were no flowerpots for something to hide behind. I began to cut the chard closest to the entry.

We were about done when something on the ground at the edge of the concrete sidewalk glinted in the sweep of my flashlight. I shined my light on it and saw what I thought was a hatpin, its jeweled top twinkling. It looked vaguely familiar. Taking a tissue from my pocket, I wrapped it and slipped it into my jacket.

I'd have to wait to examine it more carefully. I wanted to keep this to myself for now—something like this might set Ivan off again if he saw the sharp object.

We finished gathering the leaves that had cushioned Gertie's fall and went back inside. Ivan cast one more fierce look into the night and once again closed and locked the door behind us. Gertie took the basket of chard and headed to a small room off the kitchen.

"I have a soaking sink. I'll put them in there and deal with them later," she said.

I wanted to look at the pin. I went to put my coat away and pulled it out. The unusual pattern on the top looked like one I'd seen this morning. I reached for my camera to find the picture.

"Kelly, we're ready to start dinner," Stevie called out.

It would have to wait. I tucked the pin back in my jacket, put my coat on the bed, and went back to the kitchen.

Gertie returned from tending to the chard, carrying a dog bed and a bag. "I have treats for the four-legged kids, and Fred can lie on this. I keep it just for doggie guests."

Daniel took the bed and put it next to the two that were already there for the beagles. Gertie pulled three chew bones from the bag.

"This will keep them busy for a while," she said, then turned to the group. "Let's have dinner!"

The table must have been groaning. Green bean casserole with crisp onion rings on top, cranberry jelly, which I was willing to bet was homemade, piles of mashed potatoes, gravy, candied yams, dressing, and a huge platter of turkey. Everyone heaped their plates full. Indeed, a Thanksgiving feast.

"Have the Silver Sentinels solved any crimes while I was gone?" I filled my fork with tender turkey.

"Actually, we did," Mary said. "The owner of our local market approached us and asked for help. Sweet young man."

The Professor put down his fork. "He'd been having liquor bottles go missing on a regular basis. He hadn't been able to find anything by skimming his surveillance tapes. Looking at them was very time consuming, and they needed a close review."

Mary took up the story line. "We each took tapes and then met to show each other what we'd found. We discovered three young men working as a team. Because there were three of them, it was harder to spot what was going on because they provided cover for the person taking the bottles. They also traded off and at times only two would show up, so there was no pattern formed."

Gertie shook her head. "The Henderson boys and a friend. No surprise there, considering their father. He's been in and out of jail numerous times."

Mary made a sound. "They should have arrested the woman in the produce section who was pinching those poor avocados. Bruised them all. I wanted to give her a piece of my mind."

I smiled and asked, "Anything else happening?"

Ivan reached for the mashed potatoes. "They not let me enter my borscht in the Whale Frolic chowder contest."

The Professor patted his mouth with his napkin. "Ivan tried to convince them it was beet chowder, but they weren't buying it."

Everyone laughed, and Gertie said, "Just because it isn't in the contest, it doesn't mean it doesn't taste great. You're a master borscht maker, Ivan."

Ivan smiled broadly and ladled gravy on his mound of mashed potatoes.

With contented sighs, dinner came to an end. The Sentinels began to clear the dishes and insisted Daniel, Helen, the kids, and I relax. Finally, I had a chance to check for the picture of the pin. I went to the coat room, pulled out my camera, and looked at my photos. There it was. Unless there were two identical pins, the one I found had been left in a locked cabinet at the mansion.

A knock sounded on the front door, and a group greeting was given to Deputy Sheriff Stanton. I needed to get him aside and show him the pin. Grabbing my camera, I went back to the living room.

Gertie welcomed him. "Billy, I'm so glad you could make it. We have something we want to share with you, but cake first."

Gertie had set the sequence of events. Nothing was going to stop the party from going to its next celebratory step.

Helen put her work of art on the table to a chorus of *ooh*s and *ahh*s. Two miniature beagles adorned the top, one with a pink collar, the other blue. I glanced at Jack and Jill, then back at the cake. She even had the spots right. A single beeswax candle in the middle had honeycomb spiraling up the sides.

I began taking pictures. It was an event to remember.

Gertie lit the candle and an always off-tune rendition of "Happy Birthday" was sung. Stevie's dark green shirt with gold, red, and blue tie-dyed splashes looked great next to the cake. He made a wish and blew out the flame.

Helen began cutting pieces and putting them on plates. "I hope you all like chocolate cream cake."

She was kidding, right? Not like chocolate cream cake?

The *ooh*s and *ahh*s started again as people tasted the melt-in-your-mouth goodness of her creation.

Deputy Stanton put his fork down. "That was fabulous. Helen, you did a great job. Redwood Cove B and B might lose you to this new business of yours."

"Thanks, Bill. I'm glad you liked it." Helen busied herself in the kitchen.

"Gotta go. A lot to do." Deputy Sheriff Stanton stood.

Gertie picked up his dish. "Have you had dinner?"

"No. I'll catch a bite on the way back to the station."

Gertie put an empty plate on the counter. "Nonsense. We'll fix you something to take."

"No, really, don't bother—"

"William." Gertie's stern voice belied the twinkle in her eyes. "Be polite and accept the offer."

"Yes, ma'am. Thank you." The fondness in Deputy Stanton's face was clear.

Helen pulled some plastic bags from a box Gertie had put on the counter so everyone could take some leftovers. "We'll put some food together for you while you talk to Gertie about what happened this evening."

He frowned. "Something happened I should know about?"

Gertie told him the story, and Rudy handed him the notes.

Wearing an exasperated expression, Stanton said, "Why didn't you call it in?"

"Billy, the person was gone, I knew you were coming, and the officers all have so much to do. It just didn't make any sense to do that."

Stanton shook his head.

While the group cleaned up in the kitchen, I touched Stanton's arm. "I have something to show you."

I inclined my head toward the room where my coat was, and he followed me. I turned on the light, pulled the hatpin from my purse, and handed it to him in its protective tissue.

"I found this when I collected the chard damaged from Gertie's fall. It could easily have caused the marks on Gertie's hand." I showed him the photos of her scratches.

His lips formed a tight line when he saw the jagged red lines on the back of the frail hand. He inspected the piece. "I agree with you."

"There's more. I believe this is one I inventoried at the mansion this morning." I showed him the picture. "The top has a distinctive pattern. I left it locked in the cabinet. I checked, and I still have the key in my purse."

"Who else would have a key?"

"The only person I know of is Margaret Hensley."

And she was about my height.

Chapter 10

Margaret Hensley? Unlikely. An image of the designer skirt-and-jacket manager donning a bulky coat and sweatpants flashed through my mind. Highly unlikely. But the hatpin tied the attack on Gertie to Redwood Heights . . . the scene of a murder.

The deputy put the hatpin on a nightstand. "Can you think of any reason why she might do something like this?"

"Absolutely none. I don't know if she's ever even met Gertie."

Stanton reached in his pocket for his phone.

"Deputy Stanton, this pin links Gertie to the mansion." I looked at him. "Where a woman was killed today."

"You're right. I was thinking the same thing," he said. "I'd appreciate it if you'd get Stevie for me."

"Sure." I left the room as Stanton speed-dialed a number.

Gertie was resting in the living room recliner with Jill curled up in her lap. Stevie sat on the floor, leaning back on his mom's chair. Jack stretched out on the big bed Fred had been in. The basset hound pretended he fit in the little beagle's bed. The other bed is always better. Life with dogs.

"Stevie, Deputy Stanton would like to talk to you for a minute."

"Sure." Stevie stood, and we returned to the bedroom.

Deputy Stanton closed his phone as we walked in. "Stevie, I know your mom thinks this is nothing more than a purse snatching and the person is long gone. She could be right, but until we know more, I think we should be very cautious. Are you staying here tonight?"

"Yes. I always do when I'm in town. It gives us more time together."

"Good," Stanton said.

"The Sentinels are meeting at Kelly's place tomorrow, and I plan to drive her there," Stevie said.

Stanton cocked an eyebrow at me.

"One of the boxes from Redwood Heights had photos and newspaper clippings. The group plans to sort those for me," I said.

Stanton nodded. "She's covered for now, then. I'll see what I can find out."

We joined the others. The Professor and Helen had prepared containers and resealable bags of food, and they were piled high on the counter: Thanksgiving leftovers for everyone to enjoy.

Helen picked up a paper bag and handed it to Deputy Stanton. "Bill, this is for you. I put a couple of extra pieces of cake in there in case some of the other officers needed a pick-me-up this evening."

"Very thoughtful of you, Helen. I know they'll appreciate it."

Her cheeks blossomed a rosy color. "Glad to help."

Stanton left and the rest of us packed up to go. I noticed an antique butcher block in the center of the kitchen, its top uneven from years of use. I knew from the one on the ranch, the four bolts on the side connected to a through-rod, and there'd be matching hardware on the other side. The thick slabs of wood were probably maple.

"Gertie, this looks like it's been around for a while. It's an amazing piece."

Gertie was helping distribute food. "Belonged to my grandparents. My roots are Pennsylvania Dutch. Everything sturdy, long-lasting, practical . . . furnishings, equipment . . . even people."

"What about the beautiful star-patterned quilt in the bedroom?"

"Same. Sewn together over years from leftover scraps of material. Waste not, want not."

"It's a work of art."

"Thanks. It's a family heirloom."

We left with our bags of food and warm feelings of friendship. It would've been perfect if it hadn't been for the attack on Gertie.

The alarm sounded and pulled me from a deep sleep after what had mostly been a night of tossing and turning. The bloody scratches on the back of Gertie's hand had dominated the dark hours. Who had done it? Were they only after the phone? What was the connection to the mansion?

I hoped answers would be forthcoming soon. While the coffee brewed, I took a quick shower. Pouring myself a cup, I readied myself for the day. The strong black liquid gave me the energy I'd been deprived of from lack of sleep.

I'd decided the small table next to the picture windows in the main room would be a good place to begin each morning as I did my makeup. I'd placed the raven fetish there. I liked the idea of sharing the beginning of my day with him. His wisdom guiding my plans . . . if you believed in such things.

"So, Mr. Raven, anything you have to offer would be welcome."

His turquoise eye looked at me from his cocked head, but he gave no answers.

Time for breakfast. I left the room and headed for the kitchen. As soon as I entered the hallway, I caught a whiff of homemade bread, a distinctive aroma and one I loved.

Tommy was perched at the counter with his usual breakfast of fresh fruit adorning his cereal. Helen pulled loaf pans from the oven and put them on cooling racks. Fred wagged his tail, thumping the floor, but didn't move from his place near Tommy.

Helen put her hot pads down. "Good morning, Kelly."

I pulled out a stool from under the counter. "Hi, Helen." I looked down at Fred. He wagged again. "Last night was a lot of fun . . . except for what happened to Gertie."

Helen put assorted jams, honey, and peanut butter on the counter, along with a basket of sliced bread. A plate and silverware followed. "I agree. I hope they find whoever did it."

I slathered chunky peanut butter on the warm wheat bread and drizzled local honey on top. I savored a bite and followed it with a sip of dark, rich coffee.

Helen turned to Tommy. "Time for you to get to school, young man."

"Okay, Mom."

Tommy grabbed his backpack, gave his mom and Fred each a hug, and left.

I got up and put my coffee mug in the sink. "The Sentinels will be here shortly. I'd—"

Tommy burst through the door. His eyes were wide and terrified, his fright palpable. His anguished look ripped at my heart.

His mother was next to him in an instant. "Tommy, what is it?"

"Mi . . . Mi . . . Miss Kelly, your car, smashed glass . . . windows . . ."

Even though my insides froze, I got up, trying to project calm. Tears started down his cheeks.

"Everything will be okay, Tommy."

What had happened? I hurried outside and over to my Jeep. Everything appeared normal until I went to the passenger side. Fragments of glass covered the ground. Sharp shards of glass still hung in the window frame: a disturbing vision for a young boy to see . . . or for me.

Returning to the driver's side, I opened the door. Glass littered the inside, covering the seat and the dashboard. I looked in back. The boxes were gone. Why would someone want Christmas ornaments and books? I remembered the boxes weren't labeled. Was someone taking a chance there was something valuable inside? A smash-and-grab?

As I walked back to the inn, another thought occurred to me. At the meeting with Hensley and the staff, I hadn't said how many boxes I was taking, just what was in them. There'd been a lot going on at the mansion lately. Did someone think the ones in my vehicle contained the papers I'd mentioned? Was there something important in them?

I entered the kitchen area. Tommy sat on the floor rubbing Fred's ears.

"Tommy, I understand why you're so upset. All the broken glass is scary. I'm sorry you had to find it."

He continued petting Fred, his red-rimmed eyes looking at the dog.

"The good news is, it can be fixed and nothing important was taken."

Helen took out a piece of paper and a pen. "Honey, time for school. I'll write you a note about being late."

Tommy stood, got his school stuff, and took the note from his mom. He turned to me. "I'm sorry about your car, Miss Kelly."

"Thanks, Tommy. Like I said, everything will be fine."

He left for school.

Helen frowned as she cleared the table. "It makes me uncomfortable to think someone broke into your vehicle here at the inn."

"Me too. I'm glad we had the alarm put in your cottage."

Helen nodded. "It definitely makes me feel safer."

"I'll go report this to the police, call my insurance company, and get the ball rolling to get it fixed."

Helen picked up thermoses of coffee. "I've got the room ready for the Silver Sentinels. I already put some muffins in there."

"Great. They should be here any time."

Returning to my room, I took care of the phone calls. The thought of someone being on the grounds and doing the damage they did made me shudder. I looked over at the box of legal papers. Hard to imagine there might be something important in those old documents. Still . . . with all that had been happening, I decided to be safe and lock them in the oak cabinet in the B & B's office and lock that room as well.

As I completed the task, happy chattering told me the Sentinels had arrived.

Joining them in the conference room, I saw they had already started sorting clippings and photos. I received a collective greeting and smiles from all around.

Mary bustled in carrying a container and put it on the table. "Hello, everyone. Sorry I'm late."

"No problem, my dear. We just got started," the Professor said.

She took out two plastic boxes. Removing the lid from one, she placed it in the center of the table within easy reach of the busy group. A sweet smell wafted up from squares of cake topped with toasted coconut, cinnamon, and brown sugar.

"It's Pennsylvania Dutch coffee crumb cake. Please, everyone, have some." Mary handed the other container to Gertie. "I made this cake for you and Stevie, a tribute to your heritage and a thank-you for last night."

Gertie took the offering and placed it on the chair next to her. "That's very sweet of you, Mary." Gertie smiled at her. "Matches your personality. Stevie and I will enjoy it."

Mary removed her long-sleeved fleece. Its distinctive optical star pattern with eight points reminded me of a Navajo saddle blanket, as did the cream, red, and black colors.

Gertie held up a black-and-white photo of a young woman dressed in a tailored suit, high-necked white blouse, and an ascot secured with a pin. The nipped-in waist suggested a corset. The bowler she wore had a tightly rolled rim, and she carried a riding crop in her gloved hands.

"Looks like the lady of the mansion," the Professor said.

Gertie put the photo on the table. "I wonder if this was Brandon's first wife or the second. It'll be fun putting all the photos and articles together."

"Is like a jigsaw puzzle," Rudy said. "Ivan and I do each winter." Every so often a little bit of broken English popped in amid his Russian accent.

I put a key on the table. "I'd like the room locked when you're not here. You can keep this until the project's completed."

I left them to their discoveries, got my things, and headed for Redwood Heights walking at a brisk pace. The crisp air invigorated me, and I was ready to dive into the inventory. A deputy sheriff's car in front of the mansion brought yesterday's memory of finding Sylvia back full force. The upbeat feeling left.

The front door opened, and a man stepped out. I stopped in my tracks. A tall, dark, handsome man. There was a reason that description got used so much. It said it all. And I knew him. Scott Thompson, a top executive director for Resorts International. I hadn't expected this.

His face brightened with a smile when he saw me. "Kelly, hi! I heard you were helping here."

My heart raced while my mind pulled hard on the reins. Attracted to him? Yes. Ready to start another relationship? No. He came up and gave me a quick hug.

"Hi, Scott. Good to see you. I'm doing an inventory until Redwood Cove B and B is ready for visitors." My feelings were always mixed when I was around him.

"It's wonderful to see you again." His face turned serious. "Though I wish we could meet when there wasn't a tragedy involved."

"I couldn't agree more. What time did you get in?"

"Michael and I flew in around ten and went to his place."

Michael Corrigan owned a property a short distance out of town, often used as an employee retreat. It was where he stayed when in the area.

"I'm sorry to hear you were the one who found the body. That must've been disturbing."

"It was." I saw a vision of Sylvia's body slumped in the chair. How long would reliving it go on? Forever?

"I don't know what's happening this evening, but I'd love to grab a bite to eat with you if I can."

"Sure." I recalled the informal dinner and conversation we'd had the last time we got together. "I'd like that." *Maybe.*

"I'll give you a call later, and we'll see what's going on."

"Sounds good."

He smiled at me again, and his blue eyes gave me more than a casual look. "Good to see you." He reached out and gave my arm a gentle squeeze. "We'll talk soon."

He walked to the company's black Mercedes, which Corrigan stored at the small airport where he kept his plane. When he wasn't using it, the Resorts International properties had access to it for guests. I turned and entered the mansion. I felt so torn every time I saw Scott.

I went to the parlor and over to the cabinet. Unlocking it, the first thing I looked for was last night's pin. Gone. I wasn't surprised. Its design was distinctive and the likelihood there were two was about nil.

I took out my list and my camera and began to work my way through the other items. I pulled out another cushion of hatpins—black velvet trimmed with a silver braid. I froze. The centerpiece was a long hatpin with the metal thicker than the others. On top was a large egg-shaped pearl. An image of Sylvia's body once again flashed through my mind. The pearl at the center of the blood was burned into my mind.

It was the murder weapon. I was sure of it.

Chapter 11

I took a deep breath and put the cushion on top of the cabinet. The hatpin had disappeared once already, and I wasn't going to let that happen again. As I locked the display case, my gaze met the blue pillow that had borne the hatpin—the one used to attack Gertie.

I froze.

Oh, my gosh! The hatpins were from the same case. The attacker could have been the murderer.

My fingers felt like sausages as I pushed the buttons on my phone. I had to reach the Professor as quickly as possible. He'd be the calmest of the group.

"Hello, Kelly."

"Professor, I've discovered something. Is Gertie there?"

"Yes," he replied.

"Don't let her leave until I get there. I'll make it as fast as I can."

"Certainly, Kelly. I can manage that." The Professor spoke quietly. "I look forward to hearing what you found."

"Thanks, Professor." I closed my phone. I picked up the cushion and went in search of Deputy Sheriff Stanton.

I found him in the dining room, where I'd been questioned by the detectives. He was sitting at a table with an array of papers in front of him, deep in thought.

"I have the murder weapon." I thrust the pillow with the hatpin toward him. "This is it."

His head jerked up, and he reached for the cushion. "How can you be so sure?"

"Because the image of that hatpin will be with me forever."

"Okay. We'll have it tested." He examined the hatpin. "It could certainly be used to kill someone with its length and thickness. If it proves to be the murder weapon, you've helped us a lot."

"Deputy Stanton, we have to tell the Silver Sentinels. Both hatpins came from the same case, and the murderer could be Gertie's attacker."

"Ms. Jackson, this is a murder investigation—"

"If you don't tell them, I will. And Daniel needs to know, too. He's very observant. There's a chance he'll see or hear something useful."

Stanton sighed. "I can't stop you."

"They can keep a secret. I'm leaving now to meet with them at my B and B."

The deputy stood. "I'll give this to the detectives and be along shortly."

I gave him the key to the cabinet and left via the parlor, picking up my things. As I exited the mansion, I called Daniel.

"Hey, Kelly, what's up?" he answered.

"Daniel, can you meet me at Redwood Cove B and B as soon as possible?"

"Sure. What I'm doing can wait. Is everything okay?"

"Let's just say no one else has been hurt, and we need to keep it that way. That's why we need to meet."

"Got it. See you in a few."

I began to jog to the inn. A short time later, the Victorian came into view. Breathing heavily, I slowed down to catch my breath. No reason to alarm anyone more than necessary. The news itself would be enough.

The kitchen was empty. I took a quick trip to my room and looked at myself in the mirror, wanting to look as calm and together as possible. I brushed my tousled hair and took several deep breaths. A bottle of Pellegrino from the refrigerator provided a couple of cold, tingling sips of water. As soon as I felt ready, I headed for the conference room to see the Silver Sentinels. Daniel came down the hallway and joined me as I entered the conference room.

Neat piles of newspaper clippings and photos covered the table. The puzzle was beginning to be put together. Each of the Sentinels had stacks in front of them and they were putting items into labeled piles as they chatted.

Mary glanced up and then grabbed a newspaper article. "Kelly, wait until you see what we found." She held it up. "It's about—" She stopped as she took a closer look at my face. "Has something happened?"

I must not have done as good a job as I thought of getting myself together. "We need to talk."

The buzz of the busy bees stopped. The sudden silence left a void for imaginations to slip in and suspect the worst.

I explained to them what I'd found. "I believe the attack on Gertie could be much more serious than we thought. It's possible Gertie's life is in danger."

There were worried mumbles all around as the group stared at Gertie with concerned looks.

Gertie said, "Makes me all the more pleased I got a couple of good hits in with my cane."

The Professor picked up his pen and began to twirl it. "We guessed there'd been a homicide, as I shared with you yesterday. But murder with a hatpin?" He shook his head.

"It's possible. We need to see if there is any connection between Gertie and the mansion," I said.

While I'd been talking, Deputy Sheriff Stanton had arrived. He stepped forward. "Gertie, is it okay for me to see the contents of your purse?"

"Of course, Billy."

Gertie's small tan purse with a shoelace-width shoulder strap held few things. A zippered pouch contained several dollar bills and some change. A comb, mirror, tissues, a pen, lip balm, and her phone completed the list.

"May I look at your phone?" Daniel asked.

"Certainly."

He opened it and scrolled through, then held up a snapshot. "There. I wondered if you'd gotten photos of him." He looked around the group. "Robert James and the person he met with are in the background of some of the pictures Gertie took at the party for Allie. She's been helping tutor my daughter and joined us yesterday."

"A link to the mansion," the Professor said.

"Let me see." Deputy Sheriff Stanton took the phone and studied the images. "Forward the ones with him in it, and I'll put out an APB."

"Our first order of business is to find him," the Professor said.

Deputy Stanton looked at him. "How do you intend to do that?"

"Rest assured, we'll figure something out." The Professor smiled.

"Do we know for sure his name is Robert James?"

"We don't know anything for sure." Stanton went over and sat next to Gertie. "I'm concerned about your safety. I'm asking you to please not go anywhere by yourself until this is settled."

Gertie nodded. "I understand, Billy. You have a lot on your mind, and I don't want to add to your worries. I'll do as you say."

His shoulders relaxed, and he took a deep breath. Gertie was a spitfire and didn't take direction easily.

"Thank you, Gertie." He addressed the group. "I need to go. Let me know if you find out anything."

"You can count on it," the Professor replied.

Deputy Sheriff Stanton left. The Professor went to the side of the room that held meeting supplies. He pulled a piece of chart paper from a pad and picked up a felt pen.

"Let's list what we know about Robert James."

Daniel took the paper from him and attached it to the wall. "He asked me questions about the area."

The Professor wrote down he was interested in Redwood Cove. "What else?"

The group brainstormed, but the results were meager. All they added were details such as what he looked like, that he was about five seven, he wore stylish clothes, he paid in cash, and he'd stayed at a very upscale establishment—Redwood Heights.

I studied the list. "He seems to have money, and he likes nice things and places. My guess is if he's still in the area, he'd stay at a high-end place."

Gertie picked up her cell phone and punched some buttons. "I know managers or reservation clerks at four inns matching the criteria."

Mary did likewise. "My contacts number six. Some of them are in my knitting group. Let's each make a list. It'll go faster that way."

Rudy went over and tore off two sheets of chart paper. He handed one to Ivan and put the other one on the wall at one end of the table. Ivan followed suit at the other side of the room. Rudy took out two markers and tossed one to Ivan.

Gertie moved to Ivan's end of the table. "Black Swan Inn. Beth."

Ivan printed in all capital letters using large, bold strokes.

Mary joined Rudy and said, "White Water Inn. Meredith."

Delicate, cursive handwriting appeared on Rudy's list, the letters embellished with curls and swirls.

Daniel started one of his own. "I've done handyman work at a number of sites and know some people as well."

The Professor wrote on a notepad, frowning, erasing, writing again.

Heading for the door, I said, "I see you're well under way. I'll leave you to it."

The Professor stopped writing and sat back. "Kelly, wait a moment. I'd like to get your opinion as well as the others on what I wrote." The Professor looked at the Sentinels. "Everyone, could I have your attention for a moment."

The room became quiet.

"I've prepared an e-mail to send to those people who know us and are familiar with our group." He read from his paper. "The Silver Sentinels are requesting your help in solving a crime. We are looking for a man who recently registered under the name Robert James at Redwood Heights. However, he might be using a different name. We've included his picture in this e-mail. If he was at your establishment last night or is currently there, please notify us immediately. Do not let him know he's being sought. When the case is concluded, we'll send you information about what happened. We, the Silver Sentinels, thank you for any assistance you can give us."

"Excellent," Gertie said.

The other Sentinels nodded enthusiastically.

"I agree, Professor. It's well written and to the point," I said.

"Fine, then. Gertie and Mary, I'll send this to you so you can contact the people you know," the Professor said. "As soon as your lists are complete, Ivan, Rudy, and I will start writing down likely places where we don't have personal contacts."

I headed for the door. "I'll check in on you guys in a bit."

They returned to their tasks.

I went to the office and retrieved the box of legal papers. It was time to find out what was in them. Placing them on the coffee table in my quarters, I opened the box, took out a handful of documents, and began my own sorting task.

The print on the brittle, yellowed papers was still legible. I didn't understand a lot of the legal jargon, but I could get the gist of what they were about. A woman was suing the owners of Redwood Heights, claiming the property was hers as a Brandon family member. The Brandons never had children, so she wasn't a descendant. Was it a cousin who felt she had more of a right to the property than the distant half-cousins who'd inherited? I didn't know enough of their family history to have answers. The papers didn't seem important, since she must have lost the case. The place hadn't changed hands until it was sold to Resorts International.

My phone rang, and I saw it was Stanton. "Hello, Deputy Stanton."

"Hi. We don't have the results yet on the hatpin, but the detectives would like to talk with you again."

"Sure." I filled him in on what I'd found and what the Sentinels were doing.

"They're an amazing group. I wouldn't be surprised if they locate the guy before we do."

We hung up, I got my stuff, and I popped into the conference room.

More charts hung from the walls. Under Gertie's four inns, a horizontal line had been drawn and "other contacts" written. Eagle's Nest Inn—"Maria, cook" was the first entry. Columns down the right side were labeled contacted and response. Checks indicated all had been contacted. The other column noted two people had said no, and one was checking. No luck finding Robert James yet. Mary's chart was similar.

Gertie explained, "We decided to list any place where we knew people other than those involved in registration. They could connect us to who we need to talk to on a personal level."

"Daniel left to see the people he knows," the Professor said. "We've made a list of possible places where we don't know anyone."

I laughed. "That list is pretty short."

"Well," Mary said, "we've lived here a long time."

"I'm going to make copies of the man's picture and contact the establishments on that list in person," the Professor said.

Gertie piped up. "We've got lunchtime plans. Daniel's going back to where he saw Robert James yesterday."

Ivan got up and engulfed Gertie's shoulder with his large hand. "Yah. And we go to other eat places in town together."

Mary patted Rudy's hand. "And we're a team as well."

I wished them luck and left.

Helen stood at the kitchen counter putting ingredients into a mixing bowl. There would soon be some wonderful smells on the way.

She put her measuring cup down. "The tow truck driver just left with your Jeep, and the contractor working here says he has the equipment needed to clean up the glass."

"Good. I wondered how I was going to take care of that." I put on my jacket. "I have to go back to the Heights. See you later."

I grabbed the keys to the inn's truck from the hook next to the back door. The red pickup with REDWOOD COVE BED-AND-BREAKFAST on the side would be the vehicle I'd be using for a while.

The detectives had set up shop at the far end of the dining room next to Deputy Stanton's area. They were a contrasting pair. Detective Nelson wore an indigo shirt that brought out the color of his piercing blue eyes. His well-cut suit and soft leather shoes combined to make a statement. His partner, Detective Rodriguez, on the other hand, was a different story. It didn't look like his wrinkled shirt and crumpled jacket had met an iron in a while.

"I'm glad you were available." Detective Nelson came up to me. "I want to talk to my partner for a few minutes, then we have some questions for you."

"Okay." I settled into a chair, tired, worried for Gertie, wishing this was over.

He joined Detective Rodriguez on the other side of the room.

"Do you think she did it?" Detective Nelson's voice sounded in my ear as if he were standing next to me.

Startled, I looked over and saw him on the other side of the room. What was going on?

Detective Rodriguez scratched his head. "Well, she's the only one who saw the body with the pearl present, and she found the said weapon. She could have killed the victim, removed the hatpin, and hid it. There's only her word it was there when she left."

Was I going nuts? Was I imagining I could hear them? And . . . they were talking about me! I rolled my eyes and my glance stopped at the ceiling. A domed roof. My mind raced, trying to remember something from long-ago physics classes. Tantalizing memory bits came back to me. The sound was being carried over the concave surface. Unintential eavesdropping. Worked for me.

"Then why bring the hatpin to our attention?" Detective Nelson asked.

"It would appear to prove her story and, by finding it for us, she might think that clears her of suspicion."

"Maybe she *is* our murderer," the blue-eyed detective said.

What! Me?

Chapter 12

"Ms. Jackson only returned to town day before yesterday. It does seem unlikely she's the one," Detective Rodriguez said.

Detective Nelson picked up his notepad. "Maybe she knew the victim before coming here."

"Possibly. Let's see what we can find out."

As they started walking toward me, their voices faded.

Detective Rodriguez stopped in front of me. "Ms. Jackson, we have a few questions for you."

Forty-five minutes later I was leaving out the back door. They questioned me a lot about whether or not I'd known Sylvia before coming to town. They'd also quizzed me at length about the interactions I'd had with her. I knew they wouldn't find anything to connect me to her murder because I didn't do it. Still, it was unnerving to be considered a possible murder suspect.

As I passed the garage, Stevie and his four-legged dynamic duo were getting into their RV.

He looked at me and waved. "Kelly, I have a question for you."

I headed in his direction. "What's up?"

Jack and Jill bounded over to me, tails wagging, lips pulled back in doggie grins. Kneeling down, I responded to their enthusiastic greeting with ear rubs and hugs.

"I want to check the carriage house for bugs, but I know you're working in there. Will I disturb you?"

"No. Not at all. I'm going to take a couple of boxes back to my place. It's easier to inventory them there."

As we were talking, Deputy Sheriff Stanton joined us. "How's your mom doing today?" he asked Stevie.

Stevie laughed. "Other than muttering about wishing she'd gotten another whack in with her cane, she's fine."

"I'm glad to hear it." Stanton stiffened as he glanced into the motor home. "Stevie, what's that on your couch?"

"I was going to bring it over later after I gave the dogs some water." He reached in and retrieved the object that had attracted the officer's attention.

Stevie held a diamond bracelet up in the sunlight. The diamonds' fire and brilliant multicolored sparkle almost blinded me. I'd never seen one with such large stones. I guessed the red and green flashes on the clasp were rubies and emeralds, befitting of such a piece.

He held it out to Stanton and grinned. "Jill found it. I think whoever lost it is going to be very happy."

The deputy pulled out a latex glove and a plastic bag from his pocket. He put the glove on and carefully took the bracelet and dropped it into the baggie. Stevie frowned, and his grin disappeared.

Deputy Sheriff Stanton sealed the bag. "Do you have any idea where she got it?"

"I can take you to the general area. The dogs were searching under bushes next to the carriage house. I couldn't see them the entire time they were working."

"Show me where you're talking about."

"Sure." Stevie's frown hadn't gone away. "Is there something wrong, Bill?"

"There have been some jewelry thefts here recently. This looks like one of the items."

"Oh, wow. I didn't know, or I would've brought it over sooner." Stevie grabbed a couple of leashes, clipped them on the dogs' collars, and closed the motor home.

We walked in silence to where the bracelet had been found.

"I'm going to go inside and choose a couple more boxes to take back with me," I said.

Stanton looked at me. "I'd like you to stop by and see me before you leave." He turned to Stevie. "After I look this area over, I'll come by your motor home. I have some questions for you."

"No problem. The dogs and I were ready to take a break." Stevie, Jack, and Jill headed back the way we had come.

I entered the cool, dim interior of the carriage house. A few sunbeams struggled through the dusty windows. Shafts of light pierced the narrow gaps between the rafters. Switching on the light by the door, I walked over to one of the stacks of boxes.

It didn't take long to decide what I wanted. The first two I opened had more papers the Sentinels could sort. I decided to only take the third one back with me for now. It was filled with tiny cloth-wrapped objects. I uncovered the first item and held up a glass figurine much like the ones I'd been inventorying. The slightly blurred details on the face and the simplicity of the form made me think this one wasn't as high quality. A quick search of the next few items showed similar traits. This would be a good one to do in the garage.

As I stepped out of the building, a raucous cawing pulled my attention to the top of a tall tree. A large raven perched on one of the branches seemed to be telling me off. I thought of the fetish sitting in my room. Grandpa had given it to me to help in my new journey. I could sure use a lot of that now.

I walked back to Redwood Heights to check in with Stanton, touch base with Hensley, and get the truck. The interview room being empty, I went to the office. The manager was leaning back in her desk chair, eyes closed. At my knock on the door frame, Hensley opened her eyes, sat up, and straightened her jacket. There were dark circles under her eyes, and her shoulders sagged.

"Yes, Kelly, how can I help you?" An unspoken sigh between each word made the question sound slow and heavy, but her professional demeanor remained in place.

"I wanted to let you know I'm headed back to the B and B with another box . . . unless there's something I can do to help you here."

"Not right now, but thanks for asking. Michael, Scott, and I have relocated the guests to Ridley House." She paused. "Unfortunately, another piece of jewelry disappeared. I'm getting ready to question Tina again, since she cleans the rooms where things have gone missing."

"Stevie's dog Jill found a bracelet, and Deputy Sheriff Stanton thinks it might be one of the stolen pieces."

Hensley bolted upright, no more limp shoulders. "What? That bug man is involved?"

My shoulders tightened. "No, he's *not* involved. Stevie's dog retrieved it." Putting in a few points for Stevie, I said, "I'm sure the owner of the piece will be very pleased and thankful."

Our exchange ended when Tina arrived. From the grim look on Hensley's face, things didn't bode well for her. The young woman's pale, ashen face reflected her apprehension.

I went back to the interrogation area. The detectives and Stanton were on the far side of the room questioning Stevie. I stationed myself in the chair I'd used earlier—supposedly out of earshot.

They were asking him about his whereabouts on the days the thefts had taken place. He wasn't on the premises, he said, but he had no one to corroborate his story as he'd worked alone and hadn't interacted with anyone. The palms of his hands slid down his jean-covered thighs over and over. He shook his head repeatedly as they questioned him his about interactions with Mrs. Porter and the Redwood Heights staff.

"That's all the questions I have for now," Detective Nelson said.

The other two officers nodded.

"You don't think I stole those things, do you?" Stevie asked.

By the cold stares of the detectives and Stanton's frown, I'd say that was a strong possibility.

"As I said, that's all for now." Detective Nelson turned away. "Don't leave the area without checking with me."

Stevie passed me and our eyes met—his filled with fear. Beads of perspiration dotted his brow. I turned to follow him out and offer reassurance.

"Ms. Jackson," Deputy Sheriff Stanton said, calling me back. "We have a few things we'd like to ask you."

Reluctantly, I turned in their direction. They questioned me about my knowledge of Stevie, where he'd been working, and whether or not I'd seen him talking with any of the employees. I told them what little I knew and wished I could say more to help him.

After they were done, I walked back through the house to get the pickup and encountered Tina walking down the hallway, tears streaming down her face, her eyes puffy. She stopped when she saw me.

"Tina . . ."

"I hate that woman! I know I shouldn't say that, but I do," she sobbed. "She thinks I'm a thief."

"Don't worry. They'll find who did it."

"She even asked me about the Porter woman and where I was when she was killed. It's like she's trying to pin that on me, too."

"The police will get to the bottom of it."

"It's a terrible thing being suspected of something you didn't do."

Tell me about it.

She added, "And you read stories in the paper all the time about people being found innocent after spending years in jail. I read one just the other day."

Years in jail. Uh-oh.

Chapter 13

I put my hand on her forearm and gave a gentle squeeze. "Tina, they'll find out who stole the jewelry and murdered Mrs. Porter."

"The question is when," she replied. "Before I get arrested? I think Hensley's convinced I stole the stuff, and I'm sure she'd be happy to clean up what's been happening by putting the murder on me as well."

"She's not doing the investigating. It's not her call." I paused. "As best you can, put your fears in a mental box, put it aside, and trust the police to work it out. Deputy Sheriff Stanton is a fair man and not one to jump to conclusions."

Tina took a deep breath. "Okay, Kelly. That's good advice. Worrying won't make any difference."

"Think about the cooking classes and how much you enjoy them."

Tina nodded and pulled a tissue from her pocket. She wiped off the black smeared mascara that had collected under her eyes from her tears. "Thanks. I better go help get the afternoon appetizers ready for Ridley House." She gave me a grateful look and left.

Next, I needed to talk to Stevie. I walked to his RV and knocked on the door.

"Who is it?" Stevie asked.

"It's me, Kelly."

He opened the door. His face was a mottled red. The dogs were leaning on his legs and looking up at him. No wagging tails.

"I wanted to check on how you're doing."

With a slow movement, he pushed the door open wider. "Come on in."

Stevie turned. He had a multicolored cloth band around his wispy gray ponytail. I walked up the steps behind him. His home on wheels had a brown couch on the opposite wall, a dining area with booth seating on my left, and a beige vinyl chair on my right. A vine in a macramé holder hung down in the corner of the eating area.

He pointed to the chair. "Please, have a seat. Would you like some iced tea?" His voice sounded wooden and mechanical.

"That would be nice."

He got a glass from a dish rack and went to the small refrigerator. He opened it and pulled out some ice and a pitcher of tea. His movements reminded me of spaceship pilots in a weightless environment—calculated, methodical, deliberate.

His blotched face and almost catatonic demeanor worried me. What could I do to help him? I looked around the vehicle as I thought about it. I spied two dogs beds, one blue and one pink, with monogrammed names in fancy white letters. A cream-colored candle on the kitchen counter probably accounted for the faint, sweet smell of jasmine.

He handed me the tea and sank down on the couch, slumping back into the cushions. "Tell me I'm dreaming. It's all a nightmare. I'm going to wake up from this, and everything will be normal." His eyes pleaded with me. "Right?"

"Stevie, I wish I could say that was the case. I do believe there will be a time when it will all seem like a bad dream, and it'll be over."

He nodded—a weary, resigned movement. He took off his gold wire-rimmed glasses, and pulled a cloth from a drawer next to him. Slowly, methodically, he wiped the round lenses. He put the glasses in his lap and rubbed his eyes and then his face.

"The police will get it all figured out," I said

"The attack on my mom. The woman being murdered. All this craziness. What's it about?"

"I don't know, but the Silver Sentinels are working on it as well."

He gave a slight smile. "Mom loves being part of that group."

I felt a shift in emotion from him. "They serve the community and accomplish a lot. They have a right to feel proud."

He straightened his back and stretched.

"We'll get to the bottom of it," I said.

Soon, I hope. Very soon.

"Thanks, Kelly. I feel a bit better."

"Why don't you share that with your kids?"

The beagles had continued to lean on him with worried looks on their faces. Stevie patted his lap and both were on it in a nanosecond, tails wagging. He hugged them one at a time and sat back.

"Daniel told me you rescued them."

"Yes." He rubbed the back of Jill's ear, and she sank farther into his chest. "I'd been thinking about getting a dog. When a rescue group set up at a local park, I decided to stroll through the pens."

I sipped my tea and was relieved to see Stevie's face regain its normal color.

"These two were together, Jill pressing against the far side of the enclosure, trembling, with Jack at her side, watchful of the milling strangers. The group wanted to adopt them out together, but Jack was very protective, and they hadn't been successful."

"How did you manage to convince Jack to trust you?"

"I sat outside their area softly talking to them for about half an hour. Jill peeked over Jack's back. She ducked down again but looked up after another ten minutes. I decided to sing, and that did it."

"Sing?"

"Yeah, 'Where Have All the Flowers Gone' won her over, and she came to the fence and licked my hand. Jack was right beside her, watching my every move."

"It's great you were so patient."

"I got into the pen and sat on the grass, and Jill crept into my lap. Jack stayed a few feet away. I was going through every folk song I knew to get him closer. Partway through 'The Sounds of Silence' Jack decided that was his song. He wasn't ready to get in my lap, but he sat down next to me."

"And now you're a family."

"Yes, now we're a family. Jack sings with me now." Stevie sang a few lines of the Simon and Garfunkel song in a soft, mellow voice. Jack tilted his head back and crooned along with him.

We laughed, and I thought about how good the happiness felt. Stevie looked and sounded like himself again. Talking about the dogs had brought him out of his dark place. I decided to keep it going. A picture on the wall of the three of them in front of the motor home with the slogan on the side caught my eye.

"How did they become professional sniffers?"

He grinned. "It started out as something fun for us to do. I'd heard about it and wanted to see if I could train them. They were superstars at it. So . . . here we are. I travel up and down the coast. Michael has me on contract to do his properties, and I get jobs as I travel. My hours are flexible, and it allows me to spend time with my mom. I love it." He looked at his watch. "Speaking of Mom, I want to get home so I'm there when she gets back."

I finished the last of my drink and stood. "Thanks for the tea. Time for me to go, too."

"Mom always says do what you can to solve a situation and then put it aside and get on with life." Stevie looked at me. "This is a good time for me to do just that."

"Good advice." *And now I need to apply it to myself.*

"Stop by any time." He opened the door and pulled keys out of his pocket. "To the truck, Jack and Jill."

The dogs shot out of the RV and raced to a small dusty green pickup.

"See you later," I said and walked back to the mansion. Tina and Stevie seemed in a better place. *Now if someone could help me.*

I drove the pickup to the carriage house and retrieved the box. As I reached the Redwood Cove B & B parking lot, my cell phone rang. The number identified it as Scott.

"Hi." I was almost home.

"An emergency meeting's been called. We need you to come back to Redwood Heights now. We're in the office."

"Okay. No problem. See you in a few."

What had happened now? I pulled into the driveway of my place and did a U turn. I parked in front of the mansion and walked in. The three policemen, Scott, Corrigan, Daniel, and Hensley were there.

Corrigan greeted me with a quick hug. "Good to see you. Sorry we haven't had a chance to talk yet."

I returned the light embrace. "Good to see you, too, Michael."

"There's a chair over there." He pointed to one next to Detective Rodriguez.

I sat and waited.

Deputy Sheriff Stanton stood and addressed the group. "As you're aware, the dead woman was not Sylvia Porter, an employee working for Preston Insurance. We've been working to find out who she was."

Stanton looked directly at Corrigan. "Sylvia Porter was actually Mrs. Sylvia Madison. She worked for Resorts International. She worked for you, Mr. Corrigan."

Chapter 14

Stunned silence filled the room.

Corrigan sighed, shook his head, and looked at Stanton. "I didn't know her."

"I understand. I know your company is very large." The deputy looked at his notepad. "She was employed as a spotter. What did she do exactly?"

"That's someone who—"

Before Corrigan could say more, Hensley, her eyes wide, her chin jutting forward, interrupted him. "It means she was a spy! Michael, how could you? You sent her to check on me? And the staff I was responsible for? After all the years we've known each other?" Her voice shook with fury.

"Margaret, you know I have an interested buyer for Redwood Heights, and it's company policy to have places reviewed before they're sold."

"But me? You doubted I was doing my job?"

Corrigan's lips formed a tight line. "No, I didn't."

Deputy Stanton cut in. "Mr. Corrigan, you were starting to give an explanation. Go on."

"Her job was to be at a site, without anyone knowing who she was. Even me. There's one administrator who handles that department, and she's the only one who knows who those employees are."

"What kinds of things do they look for?"

"They measure staff courtesy, cleanliness of the site, and following protocol, to name a few. It's a long list. I'll write down the name and number of her supervisor for you."

"I'd appreciate that." Stanton looked at me and at the manager. "Ms.

Jackson and Mrs. Hensley, now you know the deceased woman's purpose for being here and that she was a company employee, is there anything you can think of that she said or did that has a new interpretation?"

I thought a moment, then shook my head. "No, not offhand. I'll go back through my interactions with her and let you know if I think of anything."

"Mrs. Hensley?" Stanton turned to the manager.

Would she be able to talk, considering her tightly clenched jaw?

"It explains why she was so annoying to the staff. Testing us— seeing what our limits were." She shot an angry glance at Corrigan. "I'm sure you'll find everyone did well."

Stanton tapped his pen on his notepad. "Anything else?"

The manager looked away. "I'll give it some thought, too."

"We're asking for alibis between eleven thirty, when she was last seen, and twelve forty-five, when guests began arriving in the lobby for a tour. The entrance to Sylvia's room is visible from there, and no one saw anyone enter or leave. We suspect closer to eleven thirty because she hadn't taken the nap she mentioned and the blood on her blouse had begun to dry a bit around the edges."

I shuddered at the details. Sylvia had wanted to rest and sip her hot beverage. Instead she was murdered.

Deputy Sheriff Stanton looked at the other two officers. "Do you have any questions?"

"None that I can think of at the moment," Detective Rodriguez said.

Detective Nelson nodded in agreement.

Deputy Stanton glanced around the room. "Jerry Gershwin confirmed Cindy's account of yesterday morning. Your other two live-in staff members don't have alibis." He slipped his notes into the front pocket of his shirt. "Okay, folks, that's all for now."

I got up and started for the door. Scott caught up with me. We didn't say anything until we were outside.

"That was a shocker," Scott said as we stopped next to my truck.

"I agree with you there."

"Kelly, this is a difficult situation and trying for all of us. How about we take a break from it and have dinner tonight? I'll make the long, steep, perilous hike to the grocery store." His wide grin acknowledged the joke, as it was a short, flat walk to the market. "Then I'll slave over the deli counter and put something together for us to have at your new place, Redwood Cove B and B."

A quiet night with Scott pulled at me. Maybe this was my chance to have someone help me like I'd done with Stevie and Tina. "I'd like that."

"Great!" Scott checked his watch. "I'll talk to Michael about what else needs to be done and head for the store." He turned to leave.

"See you in a bit." I hesitated. "I'm looking forward to it."

He paused on his walk back to the mansion and looked over his shoulder. "Me too."

I got into the truck. So much had happened, my mind was spinning. Hensley had been furious about Sylvia being a spy. She appeared surprised, but had she already known? She had a short fuse. Had it ignited and she killed Sylvia in a fit of rage?

Or had one of the other employees had enough of Sylvia's pushy ways? Tina didn't have an alibi for the time of the murder. Had she been fed up enough with the woman to kill her?

Jerry Gershwin's alibi had checked with Cindy's account of the day. Could someone corroborate both their alibis? They could be covering for each other. But the chef hadn't stayed there long enough to be part of the robberies if they were connected.

Then there was the attack on Gertie by someone about my height. I believed the hatpins connected the two incidents. The people similar in height to me included Hensley, Tina, Lily, and Robert James. Anyone else? The chef was a little on the short side, but the lighting hadn't been great. I kept him on the list.

Lily hadn't had a chance to take the hatpin from Sylvia's body because she was leading a tour group. Robert James wasn't a guest at the time and, to the best of everyone's knowledge, he wasn't on site. Lots of pieces weren't fitting together. A quiet night with Scott sounded perfect.

I pulled into the parking lot of Redwood Cove Bed-and-Breakfast, put the box in the shed, and entered the multipurpose room. Andy and Phil were at the counter. Andy arranged an assortment of cheese and crackers as Phil studied the labels on several bottles of wine.

"Kelly," Phil greeted me. "I just chose the wine to pair with our cheese for tonight. Do you recognize the label?"

I looked at the label featuring a delicate greyhound with a flowing red scarf, a Pegasus-like wing tucked against its side. "I do. It's from the Flying Dog winery. The sampling of their merlots you poured for me provided an educational afternoon on flights of wine."

"Cheese, cheese, cheese. Wonderful cheese," Andy sang as he unwrapped and sliced a couple of exotic-looking cheeses. "Would you like to join us?"

"Not tonight, but thanks. Scott's bringing dinner from the market, and we're going to relax a bit."

"Ahh . . . the business at the mansion. I understand. Nasty stuff." Andy shook his head.

"Did either of you have any interaction with Sylvia Porter?" I decided not to complicate matters with her real name.

Phil began to open the bottle of wine. "Very little." The cork popped as he pulled it. "She was abrasive at times but certainly nothing to kill over."

Andy put the finishing touches on his tray. "That was my experience of her as well. We were at the Heights doing some prep work for the festival. She asked me questions about cheese. At times there seemed to be a very sweet person amid her difficult demeanor."

"Thanks, guys."

Andy busied himself over a plate and then put it on the counter. "Here's a little something for you and Scott."

"How sweet of you."

The cheese monger pointed to a wedge of light yellow cheese. "Pecorino Toscano, made of sheep's milk. Many people describe it as sweet and nutty. It's PDO—protected geographical indication—meaning it has to come from a certain region in order to use the name."

I reached into the cupboard above me and pulled out crackers, along with a small wicker tray. "I'm sure it'll be delicious."

"The other one is Cantalet and AOC designated, which is basically the same as PDO. One's Italian, the other French. It's produced in Auvergne, France. Made with cow's milk. It ages wonderfully, but the wedge I brought with me isn't going to have that chance."

I lined the container with a green cotton napkin and arranged a variety of wafers in it. "It'll be a wonderful way for us to start our dinner."

Andy opened a second bottle of the Flying Dog wine. "And here's a gift from me as well."

I smiled. "Thanks."

Andy and Phil departed with their cheeses and wine for the parlor, and I set the table for Scott and me. As I was putting the napkins down, Helen, Tommy, and Fred came in.

Helen put the bag she was carrying on the granite divider. "Hi. Looks like you have plans for tonight."

"Yes, Scott's doing another market special."

"Well, that's a great place. Lots of organic and local food in what they make."

"I know. I'm looking forward to it."

"I bought a few things we need for tomorrow. I'll get them put away and then we'll go next door."

Tommy jumped onto one of the counter stools. "Did I hear you say Mr. Scott's coming over?"

"Yes, you did."

As if on cue, Scott appeared at the back door. I could see him through the window. I opened it, and he deposited a bag on the counter.

"Mr. Scott. Hi!" Tommy raced toward Scott.

"Hi to you." He gave Tommy a big hug. "And you, too," he said as Fred nosed in for his attention. His tail wagged like a furry metronome.

"Do you want to see my new Legos?" Tommy asked.

I remembered the memorable night Scott and I had spent in Helen and Tommy's cottage. Scott had been surrounded by Legos and animal posters as he was being the good sport and sleeping in Tommy's room.

"I'll pass tonight. I promise I will before I leave town."

Helen picked up her purse. "Come on, Tommy. It's time for our dinner."

They left, and Scott and I were alone.

We began to unpack the grocery bag. Scott stopped and put his arm around my shoulders. "This has been a rough time for you."

His touch felt light and warm. I glanced at him and turned away quickly from the look of care and concern in his eyes. The tiredness, the stress threatened to leap out of the place I'd been keeping it penned in and flood through my body, my mind. I took a deep breath.

Determined to keep it corralled, I stepped away, busying myself opening containers—and breaking the moment between us.

"There have definitely been some uncomfortable situations." I grabbed several serving dishes from the cabinets. "I'm glad we're doing this. Thanks for suggesting it."

Scott emptied one of the containers into a blue-and-white ceramic bowl. "The stir-fried shrimp looked particularly appealing."

I agreed with him as I placed it on the table. It was full of red and green bell peppers and what looked like shiitake mushrooms mixed in with large shrimp and a sprinkling of peanuts. A complex blend of spices filled the air. I put the brown rice and green salad next to it.

"We can't forget the fortune cookies." Scott put two on the table.

I put Andy's cheese tray out and poured glasses of the deep red merlot.

Scott picked up our glasses and handed me mine. "Here's to your new beginning at Redwood Cove Bed-and-Breakfast."

We touched glasses and took a sip. The wine had a soft, fruity flavor. "I'm so excited to be here," I said.

"I'm looking forward to hearing why you made the decision to become a manager and leave your position, which would've taken you around the world."

"Happy to share."

We served ourselves in companionable silence.

When we were settled and had begun to eat, Scott asked, "So how is it a village on the coast of California appeals more to you than trips to international resorts?"

I speared a forkful of arugula and spinach, beets, and feta cheese. "I grew up on a ranch and went to school in a small town. The town's people helped each other. There was a real community feel. I have a big, loving family, and many of the ranchers and townspeople were like extended family. I want to travel, but I want my home to be about people as well as a place."

"I had such a different life." Scott sipped his wine and sat back. "Dad worked for a large corporation, and we'd stay a year or two in one place, then we'd move. We lived overseas on several occasions."

"How was that for you in terms of friends and school?"

"I didn't develop any strong relationships with other kids. Mom always wanted the best schools for me, and a few times that meant boarding school when she couldn't find anything local that met with her approval."

"How did you feel about that?"

"I was okay with it. We went to some fun places and stayed at nice hotels while Mom was working out housing." He set his utensils down. "I love my parents, and they love me, but we're not close like a lot of families. Dad worked long hours, and Mom kept busy with all the moves."

"How often do you see them?"

"A few times a year. We usually have Christmas together."

"What's that like?"

Scott laughed. "Mom unfolds the three-foot-high white vinyl Christmas tree she got in Japan, puts it on the coffee table, decorates it with small two-inch baby blue bulbs, and makes a reservation for Christmas dinner."

I just about choked on my wine. "No real Christmas tree?"

"Nope. She'd be happy if she could figure out a way to keep the bulbs on it when she packs it up."

"And eating out?"

"She always got our reservations in early."

"What about the smell of Christmas? You breathe Christmas, not just look at it. Oh, my gosh, you missed the smell of Christmas." I was shocked someone could grow up without that special experience.

"What do you mean?"

"The scent of pine mingling with roasting turkey and pumpkin pies baking." I realized I was on a soapbox and decided I'd better get down.

"Tell me what your Christmas is like." Scott raised an eyebrow and smiled at me, faint lines crinkling around his eyes.

"Well, it's Christmas season with a special Christmas Day in it. You live Christmas with your family and friends. It encompasses weeks of neighbors coming by sharing baked goods and stories of what's happened during the year. Mom puts up two trees, a huge one in the living room and another one in the dining room. The family decorates them together. Presents pile up—mostly practical items and often handmade."

"Who's in your family?"

"I have two brothers, a sister and brother-in-law, my mom, my dad, and my grandpa. My sister had twins a few months ago, so I'm an aunt. Do you have any brothers or sisters?"

"No. There's just me."

"What are your parents doing now?"

"Dad still does some work for the company. Mom participates in fund-raising and plays bridge. They live in New York City."

I toyed with my dinner. "Have you ever thought about settling in one place for a while?"

"I've thought about it. I don't really know what that's like. This traveling position has been a perfect fit for me." He sipped his wine. "Michael has been wanting to do something more with the company retreat outside of town. He's hinted he'd be interested in me creating and handling something. We'll see."

Scott here in the area. I'd like that, even though part of me said to not get involved with someone again. I'd loved my ex-husband with the depth of a first true love and had lived with the certain knowledge we'd be together forever. The stunning sense of loss and biting pain when it came to an end was like nothing I'd experienced before. I wasn't ready to risk going through it again. I wondered if I ever would be.

Scott's phone beeped. He read for a moment. "It's Michael. He wants us all to meet tomorrow at ten."

I stood and started to pick up dishes. "I can be there."

"He talked to Sylvia's supervisor. Sylvia felt the attack on her was by the jewel thief and nothing personal regarding her. Wrong place, wrong time. She wanted to stay to see if she could help solve the crimes and felt she'd be safe by being extra vigilant."

We looked at each other.

"Poor woman," I said. "She was so wrong."

Chapter 15

Scott and I said our good nights, and I finished clearing the dishes. I stopped at the conference room and flicked on the lights. The Silver Sentinels had crossed out many of the inns and circled others in their search for Robert James. "Eight a.m. sharp" in bold red lettering topped one of the charts. I was curious to find out how the day had gone for them.

As I got ready for bed, I thought about the emotion that had started to overwhelm me at Scott's kind gesture. It seemed to have dissipated. Stevie and Tina appeared grateful for my help today. I'd hoped someone would help me—and someone did. Scott. I liked him. I liked him a lot.

There, I've admitted it. No more true confessions tonight. No more thinking about Scott.

I rolled into bed and turned off the lights.

The alarm did its job waking me at six. I opened the door into the hallway at seven and met the delicious aroma of pastries baking. Reminding myself about something called self-control, I walked a little faster.

Helen pulled a tray of croissants oozing what looked like dark purple syrup out of the oven as I entered.

"Wow! Do those smell good." I poured myself some coffee.

She placed them on cooling racks. "Thanks. They're for the Ridley House. We're keeping a sideboard of food out until late morning, in addition to the morning breakfast. Something extra under the circumstances. Luckily, I had these in the freezer."

The circumstances being Sylvia's murder and the relocation of the guests. I wondered how that was going.

"Good morning, Miss Kelly," Tommy said from his stool at the counter as he shoved his spoon in his bowl for more cereal.

Fred pulled himself up and wagged his way over for petting.

I rubbed Fred's silky ears. "Same to you, Tommy."

Helen pulled a bowl of fruit from the refrigerator, placed it in front of me, and put a basket of home-baked wheat bread on the counter. "Tommy, finish your breakfast, and I'll drop you off at school on my way to deliver these pastries."

"Okay, Mom. Can Fred come along for the ride?"

Helen tousled Tommy's light blond hair. "Sure. He's always good company."

Tommy left and returned with his backpack. Helen took the baked goods to her car, and the three of them piled in and took off. The place was suddenly quiet. Other than in my quarters, I hadn't been alone in Redwood Cove Bed-and-Breakfast for more than a few minutes since I'd returned.

I savored the moment, walking around the large multipurpose room. I already had fond memories of the interactions I had in it with my recently made friends and looked forward to many more.

A rattling engine caught my attention. I looked out the back window as the Professor's gold boat of a Mercedes sedan rocked and rolled into the yard. The dapper gentleman got out of the driver's seat, opened the back car door, and gave his hand to Gertie to help her out. Mary emerged from the other side.

I opened the back door. "Good morning."

"Same to you, my dear," the Professor said as he closed the car door.

Gertie tapped her way up the back steps, holding her cane in her bandaged hand. "We're here and ready to get to work."

"I saw your notes. I'm looking forward to hearing what you found out."

Mary came up behind Gertie, slightly breathless, plastic container in hand. "We haven't found him yet, but we feel we have good leads."

"Our dear Russian brothers will join us shortly. They do a walk each morning and decided coming here on foot would be their trek for the day."

They went to the conference room and readied themselves. I cleaned up the few dishes in the kitchen, went back to my room, and checked e-mail, then went to join them. Mary's open box occupied the middle of the table. I looked forward to what baked surprise she was treating us with today. Looking in, I saw moist-looking brownies with chunks of chocolate visible on the sides. *Right. Remember the self-control words you used this morning.*

Ivan and Rudy had joined them. The fresh ocean air clung to their clothes and filled the room.

Gertie had a variety of colored pens in front of her. At precisely eight, she picked one up and tapped the table. "Let's get started,"

The Professor smiled and turned to me. "Our first order of business is to thank you for the use of the room. It's perfect for our needs."

"You're welcome," I said.

He turned to the charts. "The inns we've crossed out have no one even remotely resembling Robert James. The circled ones have possibilities. The question marks indicate places we haven't heard from them yet."

"Yah. So this morning we do stakeout," Ivan said.

Rudy shifted in his chair. "We're going out in teams of two to the places we feel we have the best chance of finding Mr. James."

The Professor picked up his pen and began twirling it in his fingers. "Gertie's picture isn't very good. We'll take photos of the possible suspects and have Daniel look at them for identification purposes."

"It sounds like you have quite a morning planned," I said.

Mary pushed her baked goods toward me. "You need to put some weight on that slim frame of yours. These are double chocolate chunk espresso brownies." She nudged them closer. "What are you up to today?"

Chocolate and coffee together. My favorite combination. Resolve raced out the window. I picked up one of the brownies. "There's a meeting at the Heights." I savored the chocolate and coffee combination as it melted in my mouth.

Mary smiled happily as I'm sure my face reflected the divine taste of the treat. "Honey, the Whale Frolic Festival is this weekend, and it starts with a chowder competition tonight. I think you'd enjoy it."

The Professor leaned back. "Your guests will want to know about events in the area. This is your chance to learn about this one—and have a little fun. Your return has had a rocky start."

"I don't know if I can. It depends on what happens at the meeting." I sipped my strong coffee and tasted more chocolate. "I'm not sure what's expected of me tomorrow."

Gertie said, "You can buy tickets at the door. If you go, try to get there early because there'll be a long line."

"Thanks." I left them to their strategizing and went back to my room. I picked up my fanny pack, which had replaced my purse. It was so much easier to deal with when lugging boxes from the dirty carriage house.

I decided to take the truck, even though it was a short walk. I might want to bring more things back. As I arrived at the mansion, Daniel pulled in next to me. We got out and headed inside.

"How's it going at your place? Having a lot of unplanned guests isn't what you expected."

Daniel grinned. "My staff were all in the area and rallied to the situation. Friends in the remodeling business came together to finish the details. This is such a great community, and I have wonderful friends. I feel blessed."

Thoughts of my conversation with Scott flooded my mind. "It's like that where I grew up." *And I'm thrilled it's like that here.*

We said no more as we made our way to the manager's office.

The Redwood Heights staff was there as well as Corrigan and Scott. People shifted restlessly. The unknown loomed before them. Corrigan had shut the mansion to guests and a murder had been committed.

Trays of water, coffee, and juice lined one side of the office. Lily, her back to me, poured herself a glass of juice. Her long gray hair had been twisted into a knot and secured with a silver clip. She wore tan slacks and a light green smocklike top.

Tina and Cindy, dressed in blue jeans and gray sweatshirts with VEGANS ALL THE WAY printed in red on them, whispered to each other in the corner. I smiled at Scott and gave a little wave to Corrigan. Hensley sat ramrod straight at her desk. I settled in a chair near the back of the room.

Corrigan stood and addressed the group. "Hello, everyone. I have a number of reasons for calling this meeting. As you're all aware, we've had a tragic incident here involving the murder of one of our employees."

The office phone rang. Hensley pushed a button, and the ringing stopped, the call being sent to voice mail.

"The current guests have been transferred to Ridley House and will be checking out day after tomorrow." He looked at Daniel. "How is that going?"

"No complaints. They appreciate having their rooms comped. I've heard a lot of buzz about the wine and cheese pairings you're having Phil and Andy prepare for them. They're a knowledgeable group and recognize the quality of what's being provided."

"Good." Corrigan looked around the room. "We won't be accepting any reservations here at this time. I don't know how long that'll last."

Tina and Cindy exchanged worried looks. Lily frowned.

"All of you will continue to be fully employed."

I felt the waves of relief rolling across the room from the two girls in the corner.

"I've asked Margaret to prepare lists of what can be worked on during this time," Corrigan said.

Hensley nodded. "That's why I sent out the e-mail regarding wearing casual dress." She addressed the girls and Lily. "Please see me at the end of the meeting so we can discuss what I've put together."

"The two detectives will be staying here for a few nights. It takes over two hours for them to get back to their station. I offered them lodging, and they took it."

People nodded. I suspected having them on site was welcomed.

Corrigan looked around the room. "We need to get to the bottom of this. You've all been questioned by the police. Has anyone thought of anything else since the initial questioning that might be important?"

Negative head shaking indicated there were no clues there.

"Kelly, did they find out anything about your vehicle break-in?"

"They haven't contacted me. I imagine it's low on their list right now."

Corrigan nodded. "I agree. I understand you found some old legal documents in the carriage house. Is there anything there of interest?"

"I only glanced at the papers. It looks like a lawsuit. A woman claiming to be a Brandon heir. We know they didn't have any children." I glanced at Lily.

"That's correct," Lily said. "It's why the place went to distant cousins."

"Clearly the person didn't win, so the court didn't agree with her," I said.

Corrigan nodded. "I doubt there's anything there to help us, but I'd like you to review the information carefully."

"What about my inventory assignment here?"

"Concentrate on the box for now. The Heights's staff can continue where you left off."

Corrigan looked around the room. "Think hard about Sylvia's actions. Was there anything unusual in terms of how she acted as a guest?"

Tina glanced at Cindy, gulped, and said, "There was one thing." She hesitated.

"Anything, Tina." Corrigan encouraged her.

"I found her taking pictures in the pantry. She had her back to me. As I entered, I heard her dictating into her phone, something about company protocol." She shot a frightened look at the Heights's manager.

Hensley's eyes widened.

"When she saw me, she said she wanted to learn about the inner workings of a place like this. Her face was flushed, she mumbled something else, and pushed past me."

Company protocol? Was Hensley's ship not as pristine as she thought? Had Sylvia found something amiss? Had the manager found out, snapped, and killed the spotter?

Chapter 16

Hensley's nostrils flared, and she began to stand. Tina hunched down a little as if to avoid the daggers the manager's eyes threw at her. Hensley opened her mouth.

Before she could speak, Corrigan said, "I'll get in touch with her supervisor and see if Mrs. Madison reported anything." He went on without a pause, preventing Hensley from responding. "Now I want to talk about the Whale Frolic."

The manager snapped her mouth shut and sat down. The teeth grinding that I could see even at a distance foretold of expensive dental bills.

"Andy and Phil will be available to answer questions about the wine and cheese," Corrigan continued. "Kelly and Daniel, I'd like you to wear the fleece vests monogrammed with the names of your sites and have brochures available. It's an opportunity for you to promote Redwood Cove Bed-and-Breakfast and Ridley House. Lily will be in period dress and answer questions about the history of Redwood Heights."

While Corrigan discussed each person's role in the event, my mind slipped away to thoughts of Sylvia's death. Hensley clearly didn't like having the quality of her work questioned, but it was hard to visualize the designer-clad manager stabbing Sylvia. Disagree vehemently with a report, yes. But murder? No.

Then again, what did murderers look like? How did they act? Like Deputy Stanton said, "If criminals looked like crooks, my job would be a piece of cake." I let it go and tuned back in to the meeting.

"Tina and Cindy are preparing raw food appetizers," Corrigan said.

Cindy nodded. "We're excited to show people what can be created from raw ingredients."

Corrigan continued, "The crowds tend to come in groups. While Andy and Phil will be in charge of pouring the wine, we'll all pitch in if necessary."

"Where will the event be set up?" I asked.

"We're putting it on the side porch. That's close to the kitchen, and that room has limited access to the main house. We don't want anyone to wander into the building," Corrigan replied.

My phone vibrated. I pulled it out of my pocket and glanced at the screen. There was a text from Stevie asking me to call him right away. I wondered what was up.

"Does anyone have any questions?" Corrigan asked.

No one did.

"Okay, then," Corrigan said. "Scott and I are going to stay here and meet with Margaret. I know you all have plenty to do. I'll see you tomorrow."

I stood and Hensley gave lists to Tina, Cindy, and Lily. Anxious to call Stevie, I hurried out, punching in his number.

He answered right away. "Kelly, I found something strange. You need to see it. I'm at the back of the mansion."

"Okay. I'm on my way."

When I got there, I found Stevie down on his belly peering into a small hole in the side of the building with his flashlight. The two beagles were on either side of him, pushing their heads against his, eager to see what he was looking at. A massive leather tool belt rested on the ground beside him.

"Hi, Stevie," I said. "What did you find?"

"Come look." He gestured at the opening with his flashlight. "There's dry rot here, so I poked some of it out with my screwdriver."

I got down beside him.

"Sorry. You'll have to lie down on your stomach to see it."

"No problem. These are my going-to-get-dirty clothes. There's no way to stay even remotely clean working in the carriage house."

He handed me his flashlight, and I lay down on the grass. Peering into the opening, I saw the beam traveled to another wall a few inches away. Splintered wood sat along the bottom.

"I went inside the building to inspect the damage on the other side of the wall. I should've found dry rot in the pantry. It wasn't there."

I sat up, and Jack and Jill took advantage of the opportunity to rub up against me. Their warm bodies pressed into my leg, and I petted each in turn.

"What does that mean?" I asked.

"I'm not sure, other than the wall on the inside isn't the one you see in the light from the flashlight."

We both stood.

"How can that be?" I asked. "Is there a double wall here for some reason?"

"I don't know. I called you as soon as I found it."

"Do you have a tape measure?"

Stevie picked up his belt and handed me a metal measuring tape.

"That's quite a piece of equipment you have for carrying around the tools of your trade," I said as he put it on.

"Thanks. I bought the leather and designed it after a carpenter's belt. A friend of mine sewed it together. Makes it much easier working with the dogs than lugging around a toolbox."

The number of items he carried around his waist was impressive. Rolled-up leashes, a bag labeled TREATS, and a flashlight in a loop attached to the belt next to his screwdriver. There were other bags and tools as well.

"Let's measure the distance from the back of the house to the beginning of the pantry so we can get an idea of how wide the area is between the inside and outside walls."

He pulled the leashes off his belt. "I need to tie up Jack and Jill." He took treats out of the pouch and fed them to the dogs as he clipped on the leads.

We walked together to a sturdy bush, and he secured the dogs.

On the way back to the mansion, I asked, "Did you do the macramé in your RV?"

"Yes. I like doing things with my hands. Mom and Dad were self-reliant, and growing up, I helped with whatever needed to be done. I helped Dad build a garage. Mom made most of our clothes, and she could swing a pretty mean hammer."

I laughed, imagining Gertie pounding away.

"She grew all of our vegetables. She still has a great garden, and she's been thinking about getting some chickens."

"None of that surprises me about your mom. She's an incredible lady."

We'd reached the house. Measuring proved to be one of those things easier said than done. The laundry room occupied the back of the house. Stevie stood next to the washing machine, and I squeezed myself into a narrow space between open metal shelves and the wall. We got the measurements, and Stevie jotted them into a notepad he pulled from his belt. Next came the kitchen. Hoisting myself onto a counter, I held the tape flush with a window. Stevie went to the other side, and we held it over the stove.

After Stevie measured the doorways to both rooms, we repeated the process in the pantry after I moved a few cereal boxes.

Stevie began writing. "Give me a sec, and I'll tell you what the difference is."

I looked around the pantry, where Sylvia had been taking pictures. Everything appeared clean and organized to the nth degree. Stevie had moved containers away from the baseboards, and I saw no signs of damage. Considering how severe the wood rot I'd seen outside was, I would've expected something to show.

"Wow!" Stevie exclaimed. "Kelly, the difference is three feet!"

"That's a lot. Let's measure the rest of the rooms on this side and see what we get."

A walk-in linen closet, followed by a housekeeping office, yielded the same measurements as the pantry. I noted guest rooms were above the rooms we were measuring, including Sylvia's. We went into the front parlor. The multitude of windows framed the towering redwoods and flowering bushes filled with red and yellow blossoms. This measurement was the same as the one in the washroom and kitchen.

I went to the corner that connected with the back wall of the mansion. A guest computer station had been put together in that space with a cherry bookcase beside it.

Stevie walked up next to me. "I wonder what's behind that portion of wall."

"Let's go back to the washroom. Maybe we can find something there."

As we walked down the hallway, a thought hit me. "I think I know what we'll find," I said to Stevie.

When we got to the laundry room, I tapped along the wall, starting from the back. A little more than three feet in, the sound changed.

"I hear a difference," Stevie said.

"So do I."

A large corkboard with a calendar pinned to it concealed the upper portion of the area I'd tested. I removed it and handed it to Stevie.

Wood paneling covered this section. I examined the area where a doorknob should be and saw two very thin horizontal lines about four inches long, and a vertical line connecting them. I put my fingers around the edge of the paneling at that spot and pulled.

It opened, revealing a metal latch. I started to reach for it, then remembered about fingerprints. There *was* a murder investigation going on. The metal shelves held cleaning supplies and a box of general purpose latex gloves, as I had hoped. I slipped a pair on and pulled the latch. The panel swung open, revealing a gaping black hole.

"You found a door. Cool!" Stevie exclaimed.

I turned to Stevie. "This place is built like an old European mansion. The upper society wanted to be taken care of by their servants but didn't want to see them. Many places had servants' passageways. I think that's what we're seeing here."

My history buff ex had dragged me through a number of them on our honeymoon. He loved them; I hated the dark, musty places.

"Kelly, this must be how the jewel thief got in. I can't wait to tell the police. This will clear me."

I hated to disillusion him, but I remembered the conversation I'd heard about the officers suspecting me. "Maybe. Then again they might think you knew about it all along."

"But I didn't." He looked shocked at the thought.

"I know. But they're police. They need to consider all possibilities." His crestfallen look tugged at my heart. "It's a huge step in the investigation. Hopefully, it'll help them find the thief sooner."

He nodded, the happy smile no longer there. "I'll take the dogs to the motor home and go tell them."

"They're working in the interview room."

I turned and stared into the pitch-black passageway. It could explain a lot of things: how the jewel thefts occurred, the quick disappearance of Sylvia's attacker on the stairs . . . and how the hatpin vanished.

But it didn't provide an answer as to who was responsible.

Chapter 17

Pulling my flashlight out of my fanny pack, I surveyed the floor for footprints. There were none on the almost dust-free wooden surface. Dirt pockets along the sides told me someone had wiped the floors clean, missing a few areas. They wouldn't worry about footprints that close to the wall. I took off my shoes and put them beside the door, not wanting to leave tracks if that became a problem farther down the passageway. Taking a deep breath, I stepped inside.

I aimed the beam along the bottom of the outside wall and found the rotted wood that had instigated the search. I pulled out my phone and took a picture. It would need to be attended to at some point.

My light caught the bottom of a set of stairs on my right. These, too, had been wiped clean. I went up the steep incline and found doors on either side of the landing at the top. Looking at the one on my left, I found a dead bolt. Sliding it back, I pulled on the handle, and the door opened to a guest room.

I walked in, closed the door, and turned to see what it looked like from that side. There was another wood-paneled wall decorated with paintings of bucolic scenes and a fireplace to the right of it. That was the door.

As I'd done earlier, I examined the area where I'd expect to find a doorknob and found nothing. Then I slid my hand down the edge of the panel. There was a groove with enough room for my fingers to fit. I pulled, and the door opened.

There should be an inside bolt to assure privacy for the occupant of the room. Not finding anything at the top or the bottom of the panel, I turned to the fireplace. Under the mantel shelf, I found a metal rod that slid out to block the door. Simple and effective.

The paneling was a few feet wide. Where it stopped, wallpaper started. There didn't need to be a seam in the wood for the door. There was a natural change from wood to plastered wall. A clever design.

Looking at the room on the other side of the landing, I discovered the same pattern. Descending the stairs, I continued down the hallway, my light illuminating very little of the pitch black. The heavy, thick air made it difficult to breathe.

The servants' ghosts walked with me down the coal black passageway—me with my flashlight, them with a flickering candle threatening to go out and leave them in total darkness. Water sloshed in the buckets they carried to fill the lady's washbasin. A bundle of wood thudded against the wall on its way to heat the lord's room.

I shuddered as the walls pushed in on me. Stopping, I took a few deep breaths and shoved the eerie thoughts away, willing myself to concentrate. I was in a California mansion, not a medieval castle. There might be something here to clear me and the others from being suspects. I walked on, found another staircase, but kept going to where I knew there'd be a third one. This was where Sylvia's room would be.

I decided to go to the end of the hallway, leaving Sylvia's room for last. The door there was the same as the others, only I knew it wouldn't open because of the bookcase and computer station beyond. Having no reason to procrastinate further, except for feelings of dread, I ascended the staircase.

I went to the room on my right first, dreading entering Sylvia's room again. Same story in guest room number five. Time for Sylvia's. I unlatched the door and entered. The covers on her bed were still turned back, waiting for her to take a nap. Now she was in a sleep from which she'd never awaken.

Shuddering, my gaze went to the chair where I'd found her. The image of her body filled my mind. Why hadn't she screamed? Or had she and no one heard her? There'd been no sign of a struggle. Why hadn't she fought? She said she'd wanted to take a nap. She'd readied the bed. Why was she sitting in the chair? Why did the murderer come back to remove the pin? Why not take it after stabbing Sylvia?

I turned away. Her personal belongings had been removed. There was no crime scene tape because it barred the outside of the room. Time to go. Hopefully the discovery of the hidden entrance would give the police new information.

Closing the door to her room, I headed back down the stairs. I hated going down the servants' path, the dirt and the darkness, and how it brought to mind what their lives had been like—the extreme class system they'd been part of.

Keeping my flashlight aimed at the floor, I glanced up and could see the light of the doorway at the end of the passageway. I quickened my pace, anxious to get out of the darkness. Suddenly, the light disappeared. Solid black ahead.

Someone has closed the door.

I froze, my heart pounding so loudly I thought it would echo off the walls. I was scared to bring the light up and see who or what was there. The murderer must have used this passageway. Had he or she come back?

A light flashed on, the beam shone directly in my eyes. I winced and turned my head, blinded by the brightness.

"Ms. Jackson, what are you doing in here?" Deputy Sheriff Stanton demanded.

My knees almost buckled with relief. Then I thought about his question. What *was* I doing in here?

"I . . . I . . . it seemed to be the right thing to do. I checked for footprints, but the floor was wiped clean. I . . . I . . . wore gloves."

"Let's go outside." In the washroom he frowned at me and shook his head. "Ms. Jackson, if you find anything in the future that's of interest, don't proceed to investigate on your own. Wait for us."

A fair request. "Okay."

The frown remained. "Did you find anything I should know about?"

"Nothing unusual. The rooms are locked with dead bolts on the outside. There's a way to secure them from inside the room if you know the metal rod is there."

He gave me a skeptical look, turned away, and entered the servants' passageway. Relieved to be out of the stifling hallway, I put my shoes on and stepped into the kitchen. The brightly lit room was a pleasure after all the darkness. Tina was preparing food. Colorful appetizers filled several trays.

"These look really good. Are they all made with raw vegetables?"

She smiled at me. "Absolutely."

"I think of raw food as carrot sticks and sliced cucumbers."

She laughed. "You're not alone."

I pointed to mushrooms filled with what looked like cheese. "This looks like dairy."

"I know. People are really surprised when they learn you can make a cheeselike product from nuts, like almonds and cashews."

"You definitely could've fooled me. What's in this recipe?"

"Portobello mushrooms stuffed with almond 'cheese' and walnut pesto. It'll be garnished with chopped Italian parsley."

Tina transferred quarter-size, almost transparent chips into a bowl. "These are made from zucchini. The school let us use their dehydrator." Tina covered the container with plastic wrap. "So, what's going on in the washroom?"

"What I think is good news for you and Stevie. We discovered a hidden servants' passageway providing access to the rooms where the jewelry was taken. The police have new information to focus their investigation on that doesn't involve the two of you."

"Oh, thank you for telling me. This is great! That's my second piece of good news today." Her face flushed, and she began taking dishes to the sink. She chattered on like a bird twittering at a feeder full of fresh seed. "My first was Jerry Gershwin, the celebrity chef, has signed up to attend the raw cooking school with us. He's going . . ."

She stopped and stared at me, clasping her hand over her mouth, her eyes wide. "I wasn't supposed to tell anyone. Kelly, promise me you won't say anything."

"No problem. But why aren't you supposed to mention it?"

"His nickname is the Meat King. That's what he cooks on his television program. Ranchers love him and are his biggest sponsors. He's afraid he'll lose them if they know he's at a raw cooking school."

"I can understand that."

"And his ratings could go down if viewers found out and it seemed like he was turning away from meat."

That all made sense to me.

"He'd asked Cindy and me about the class we were taking. When I got sick, I knew I was going to miss a session. I checked with the school, and they said it was okay for him to take my place. His cell phone number was in his registration information. I left him a message and when he got back from the tour, he called and said he'd enjoy taking the class. Cindy was at the school getting supplies. I texted her, and she was really excited to know she'd have a chance to meet him."

The day she was sick? That was the day Sylvia was killed.

She put the last tray away and wiped her hands on a green kitchen towel. "I want to go tell Cindy the good news. See you later." She hurried out to find her friend.

I walked down the hallway, thinking about what I'd learned. Cindy had said she'd met him the morning of the murder and the time they spent together gave them alibis. He had corroborated what she told the police. According to what Tina texted Cindy, she hadn't met Jerry yet. Cindy and Jerry had lied. It meant their alibis just went out the window. They could've killed Sylvia.

Chapter 18

I needed to tell Deputy Sheriff Stanton. I'd promised Tina I wouldn't say anything, but that was before I realized her information wiped out Jerry Gershwin's alibi as well as Cindy's. Maybe he'd give me a few brownie points, and it would help make up for the passageway incident. I hit his contact button on my phone and waited for him to answer.

"Hello, Ms. Jackson. How can I help you?"

I explained what I'd learned and what it meant concerning the two alibis.

"That's helpful, Ms. Jackson," Deputy Sheriff Stanton said. "I appreciate the information."

"Deputy Stanton, I said I wouldn't tell anyone. Given what I found out, I knew I had to say something. But . . ."

"Go on, Ms. Jackson."

"I'd hate to see Jerry's reputation impacted or, worse yet, something happen to his television show, if he isn't guilty of killing Sylvia."

"What are you suggesting?"

"Please don't tell anyone about Jerry attending the raw cooking school unless you have to."

"Good point. I've seen innocent people's lives take a negative hit during an investigation, through no fault of their own. I'll keep what you said in mind."

I ended the call and put Jerry back on the list of suspects, along with Hensley, Tina, Lily, and Robert James. Cindy was too short for the attack on Gertie, but since she'd lost her alibi along with Jerry, she still had the opportunity to kill Sylvia. I didn't envy Stanton his job. None of those people seemed to be likely possibilities to me. I went to the manager's office and knocked on the door.

"Come in," Hensley said.

Corrigan and Scott were seated by the manager's desk, notepads open.

My boss stood, grabbed a chair, and put it next to him. "Here you go." He smiled at me. "Good work on the servants' passageway."

Sitting down, I said, "Thanks. I stopped by to see if you'd heard about the discovery."

"Deputy Stanton came by. Wanted to know if we knew anything about it—which we didn't," Corrigan said.

Scott leaned forward. "How did you find the passageway?"

I explained what Stevie and I had done. "Stevie and his dog team deserve credit for finding the dry rot that led to the discovery."

Hensley arched an eyebrow and busied herself arranging papers on her desk.

It was clear to me she was bound and determined not to acknowledge Stevie in any kind of positive way.

"What made you think of a servants' passageway?" Scott asked.

I hesitated a moment. "My ex-husband was a college history professor. He was passionate about the subject, and we explored a lot of mansions, castles, and museums in Europe. The homes of the lords and ladies often had a setup like the one here."

They don't need to know it was on our honeymoon.

Corrigan closed his leather-bound notebook. "Well, good work. Hopefully, it'll give the police some further clues."

Hensley spoke up. "It'll be a pleasure when they're done with the investigation and are gone."

It'll be a pleasure when they find Sylvia's murderer . . . and he or she is brought to justice.

"That's it for today, folks." Corrigan stood. "We all have our part to do next."

"Do you need me for anything here this afternoon or evening?" I asked.

"No," Corrigan said. "As we discussed this morning, I'd like you to work on the legal documents you found."

I got up, too. "Shall do."

Scott and I walked out together. The brisk ocean air was a pleasure to feel after the closed-in passageway from this morning.

"I enjoyed last night," Scott said.

"Same here. Thanks for the excellent choices for dinner."

He stopped by my pickup truck. "You're welcome."

The sun glinted off of his pitch-black hair, which emphasized his light blue eyes.

Taking my keys out of my pocket, I asked, "What nationality are you?"

"Irish. Contrary to popular belief, many people have my coloring there. They aren't all redheads like you. I'm guessing we share a common heritage."

"Actually, I'm mostly Norwegian, with a little English thrown in."

"So much for assumptions," he said, and we shared a laugh

I opened the truck door. "What do you have planned for the afternoon?"

"Michael asked me to do some work on the sale of Redwood Heights. The investigation doesn't keep that from happening."

"How soon before it'll be finalized?"

"It's supposed to close Sunday. Michael and I were planning to come down Friday." He paused. "There is some good news. The new owner wants us to keep managing for a while and plans to retain the staff."

"I'm sure the employees will be glad to hear that."

"By the way, I left my sunglasses at your place. When would be a good time to stop by and get them?"

"I'm headed back to the B and B now."

"I'll go get some paperwork I need and be over shortly."

He left for the house, and I started the truck and drove back to the inn. As I entered the back door, my stomach told me it was lunchtime. I pulled a package of sliced turkey from the refrigerator and put it on the counter, along with condiments. Crunching gravel announced the arrival of a car. A few minutes later Scott entered.

"Hi. I was just starting to make a sandwich. Would you like one?"

Scott glanced at his watch. "Sure. I have an hour before my appointment this afternoon. Let me help."

I placed tomatoes, lettuce, and bread next to the other items, pulled down some plates, and we worked together to make our lunch. I noticed the fortune cookies from last night.

I suggested, "Let's have fortune cookie appetizers and see what the future holds."

Scott picked up his sunglasses from the counter and tucked them into an inside jacket pocket. "Sounds good to me."

"You pick."

"Okay, but you need to read yours first." He reached for one, and I took the other.

"Deal." Pulling it open, I plucked out the strip of paper and read, "Your dream will come true."

"What's your dream?" he asked.

"To find my place in life, a career." I put the paper down. "It should be in present tense, because it's come true."

"Nice. I'm happy for you." He cracked his apart. "Now you can find another dream."

"What does yours say?"

"Be open to new paths."

"Maybe you're meant to work on the project Michael's been talking to you about."

"Possibly. We're having dinner tonight to discuss it some more."

"Well, I wish you the best." I picked up our plates and put them on the table. "Time for lunch. What would you like to drink? There's iced tea, or I could make some coffee."

"Tea's fine."

I poured drinks and put the glasses on the table. We settled in to enjoy our meal.

Scott sipped his tea. "You said you were looking for a place to fit in. It sounds like that was a challenge for you. I thought your family's ranch met that goal for you."

"I love the ranch, and Mom and Dad wanted me to stay there and work, like the rest of the family, but I felt driven to find something of my own, a career. After several unsuccessful experiences, I was worried I'd never find the right fit."

"What were some of the jobs you tried?" Scott took a bite of his sandwich.

"I taught middle school while I was married. Liked the kids. Didn't like a schedule with times like six minutes after nine."

"I wouldn't like that, either."

"After my divorce, I went back to the ranch for a while."

We ate our lunch, and I told him about some of my failed attempts, finishing with, "It was a long four years before arriving here."

"Are you comfortable talking about what happened to end your marriage?"

I shrugged. "He fell out of love with me and fell in love with one of my friends. She shared his fascination with history. It happens, it hurts, you move on."

"Where are you now in terms of how you feel?"

"Healed. Pretty much. Wanting to concentrate on my job right now. What about you? Have you been married?"

"No. My work doesn't support a serious relationship, much less a marriage." He looked at the clock over the stove. "I'd better get going in a few minutes. Let me help with the dishes."

He rinsed, and I put them in the dishwasher.

"The Sentinels said the chowder competition tonight is a lot of fun. I'm attending, unless I find something in the box of documents that changes my plans. Do you want to go? It starts at five thirty."

He smiled. "I could for a little while before I meet Michael."

"I'll call later and touch base with you."

"Okay. Chowder contest. Sounds like the quintessential event for your 'village' atmosphere."

"I expect so."

He left, and I went to give the musty legal documents a thorough review. I'd only glanced at them the other day, noting the suit was a little more than fifty years old. When I got to my room, I pulled a notebook from the desk, got a pen, and poured myself a glass of Pellegrino.

A couple of hours later, I stood and stretched. What had I learned? A woman named Iris Reynolds sued the Brandon estate, claiming to be the heiress of the mansion. She was a resident of New York. I listed as many names, addresses, and dates as I could find, including the attorney she consulted in Manhattan. Time to get on the Internet.

I started with the attorney. Nothing. Then I began on the list I'd generated. A convoluted, technology-driven trail later, I had the name and number of a relative.

Electrified by my find, I grabbed my phone and called.

"Evans Residential Care. May I help you?" a voice inquired.

"I hope so. I'm looking for Henrietta Reynolds. Can you help me?" I asked.

"Please hold." I was put into the telephone netherworld.

"Hello," barked a voice with the pitch of a toy poodle.

"Ms. Reynolds?"

"Miss." She strung the word out like steam escaping from a kettle. "I don't take to any of that modern foolishness."

"Miss Reynolds, my name is Kelly Jackson. I work at Redwood Heights in California. Perhaps you've heard of it?"

"No." Strained breathing in the receiver. "And call me Henry. Everyone does. Easier on my ears and your voice."

"I'd like to talk to you about Iris Reynolds."

"Why?" snapped the creaky voice.

"We found some documents with her name on them. I believe you're a relative of hers. Am I right?"

"Yep. Can't deny it."

I stopped for a moment, hesitant to bring in the word *lawsuit*. People often shied away from talking about legal issues. I scrambled to think of a reason for calling.

"Are you still there?" an annoyed voice asked.

"We're compiling a history of the manor and thought your family might be able to help us. Her name has come up, and we can't figure out how she fits into things. My boss is a stickler for accuracy and wants me to find out." Corrigan wanted answers. I didn't think he'd mind what I'd just said.

"I really can't tell you much about her. They didn't live that far away, but it could've been hundreds of miles for all we ever saw them." A sniff traveled over the line. "We only saw each other at family gatherings, the ones you pretty much had to go to. Even though she was kin, I didn't care for her a whole bunch. Always puttin' on airs. Acted like she was better than the rest of us."

"Where is she now?"

"Oh, she's done gone," wheezed Henry.

"Where to?"

"What I meant is, she's dead, girl." Exasperation filled the voice.

"I'm sorry to ask so many questions, but it's important. Can you tell me how she died?"

"Well, her family said the life just seemed to go out of her when she came home after the California thing. She just wasted away to nothin' and died."

"What was the California thing?"

A long sigh. "You see, she was convinced she was supposed to inherit some big fortune out in California. Maybe had to do with your place. Used to brag to us how she could prove it, and one day she would. She finally got enough money together, hired a lawyer, and went out west." A coughing spasm interrupted the conversation.

I waited for the wavering voice to go on. It didn't.

"Henry, then what happened?"

"She lost the case."

"Are any of her family members left besides you?"

"Nope. Leastways, not the ones she grew up with. That side of the family never was a strong bunch."

"Did she have any children?"

"Yep. Three. Humph. Used to dress those kids of hers up and talk to them about the proper manners to be used at the manor. They lived in a little shack of a place. Ridiculous."

"Do you know where the children are now? Is her husband still alive?"

"Which one do you want me to answer, girl? It's not like I can say two things at once."

I took a deep breath. "Is her husband still alive?"

"No. Boozin' son-of-a-gun. Died in a car accident when the littlest kid was only eight months old. She went back to usin' the family name."

"What about the children?"

"I don't know nothin' about them. Other side of the family raised them. They were grown when the rest of the family died off. Just disappeared."

I heard a loud chiming in the background.

"I gotta go. They're servin' dinner. If you're at the back of the line around here, you don't get much."

I rested my forehead in my hand. "Henry, thank you so much for your time. I really appreciate it. Oh, wait, one other thing. Were the children boys or girls?"

"Both. Two boys and a girl. I gotta go."

"If you think of anything else, please call me collect." I gave her the number but doubted the woman was writing it down. I thought fast. "There's a reward for whoever helps me figure this out," I said. I heard rustling sounds.

"What was the number again?"

I repeated it and winced as Henry's phone slammed down. Anybody in the way of the food line had better watch out.

I leaned back on the window seat. What had I learned? There was at least one cranky relative left, that was for sure. Iris Reynolds, who sued the Brandons, was dead. She had three children who'd been brought up believing Redwood Heights belonged to them. Their ages could be a match for Hensley and Lily. There could be grandchildren, which would put Cindy, Tina, and maybe Jerry in the running. I didn't know enough about Robert James to place him on one list or the other.

No new lawsuit had been started, so that would mean there was no compelling evidence of ownership of the mansion. It still came back to why kill Sylvia, a hotel spotter? What did she know or have that someone would murder for?

Chapter 19

There wasn't any more for me to do regarding the box. Tomorrow I'd go to the carriage house and see if I could find more paperwork regarding the lawsuit. The clock read four. The chowder competition sounded fun, and I had time to make it.

I called Scott. "Hi. I'm done with the papers. Do you still want to go to the Whale Frolic event?"

"Sure."

"Gertie said the line is long if you don't have tickets, so we should go early."

"I can take care of the tickets. I have to go by the town hall, where it's being held, on my way back to Redwood Heights."

"Thanks. See you there at five thirty."

"Okay."

So, let's see. A list of Scott's attributes. Thoughtful. Helps in the kitchen. Always polite. I shook my head. *Stop it. This isn't helping me keep my distance.* I decided to go to the multipurpose room and change the subject in my mind.

Tommy and Allie had papers spread out over the top of the oak table. Fred's head rested on Tommy's shoe, and his back paw touched Allie's foot. He wagged a greeting but didn't move other than that. Helen and Daniel sat at the counter, cups of coffee in front of them.

I walked over to the table. "Hi, kids. What are you working on?"

Tommy looked at me. "It's a project for school. Allie and I aren't in the same grade, but the school has the same theme for everyone. We have different assignments, but we can still help each other."

Allie joined in. "We're learning about whales. I didn't realize how smart they are. It's fun." She stopped, a surprised look on her face.

I think she'd startled herself. School being fun wasn't what anyone would have heard from Allie a few months ago. Back then she'd been struggling both with school and home life. Her mom had walked out on her and Daniel. Getting in trouble had been happening regularly.

Tommy's help, along with Gertie's, had turned around her grades. I guessed Gertie threw in some motherly advice as well. It was heart lifting to see the change.

"Miss Kelly," Tommy asked, "is it all right to leave the papers out over the weekend?"

"It's okay with me if it is with your mom. I won't be using the table."

Helen nodded. "That's fine. Kelly, come join us. I made fresh coffee."

"I'd love some," I said, taking the seat next to her.

Helen took a mug off a hook and poured dark, steaming liquid from a carafe. "Do you still like it black?"

"I do." I took the mug, gave an appreciative sniff, and sipped.

Daniel leaned against the counter. "We're going to head over to the chowder competition in a bit. Are you going?"

"I am. The Sentinels said it's a lot of fun."

"It is. The chefs at the local restaurants get very creative trying to outdo each other."

Helen poured herself more coffee. "The samples are small so there's not really enough to make a meal. They sell food there, and that's what we're all going to do for dinner."

"Thanks for letting me know."

We chatted a bit and then I went back to my room to change. I was still wearing my carriage house clothes, as I had now named them, having left them on as I sorted through the box of legal papers. I was ready to put on something clean.

This was a jeans-and-fleece town. My kind of place. I faced the big decision on whether to wear blue denim or black jeans and decided on black. I chose a light blue turtleneck that would match the Redwood Cove B & B embroidery on my black fleece. Black-on-black. Wasn't that considered dressy? Twisting my hair in a knot, I clipped it into place and switched the contents of my fanny pack to my purse. I was ready to go out.

I arrived at the town hall a few minutes before five thirty. There were two lines—one to buy tickets and another for those who already had theirs. I saw Scott in the latter line and joined him.

"I'm glad you were able to get tickets."

"Me too."

The doors opened and our line filed in. We traded our tickets for a chowder-voting sheet and entered a cavernous room filled with savory smells. Men and women wearing white aprons and signature chef's hats lined one wall, hovering over enormous metal containers on hot plates. People all but sprinted for them. Scott and I went to the closest one and were handed paper cups half full of creamy, steaming soup. The label on the table said CREOLE SHRIMP AND CORN CHOWDER.

Pieces of shrimp and kernels of corn filled the rich, thick broth. There was nothing low-calorie about this dish, and I didn't care. We made our way down the line, then took a breather to walk around and look at the local crafts being displayed. People laughed, joked, and compared notes on their favorite soups.

"You talked about the sense of community in a small town." Scott looked around. "I understand what you were saying in the camaraderie I see here. We never stayed in one place long enough to develop close relationships with people."

"What do you think about it?"

"It looks special. It's not something I've experienced." He sampled a spoonful of chowder. "What do people do in places like this when they're not working? In big cities there's always a long list of choices."

I pointed to the tables holding homemade white crocheted doilies, pot holders, and a myriad of other items. "Many get a hobby." There was a table with birdhouses built to look like two-story homes from the 1800s. "You could build those."

Scott looked at me with a you've-got-to-be-kidding look. "Right." He pointed to the pot holders. "It'd make more sense if I made some of those."

I laughed. "Pot holders? Why?"

"I have a hobby of sorts." He took another taste of chowder. "Hmmm. I think I detect a hint of lemongrass and maybe some saffron."

While I was impressed with his food knowledge, I wanted to know what he did for fun.

I persisted. "What's your hobby?"

"I cook." He flashed me a big grin, knowing he'd caught me by surprise. "I can whip up a mean crepe filled with Brie, basil pesto, and chopped tomatoes."

A feather would've knocked me over. "What got you interested in that?"

"I eat out so much, I decided when I was home, I wanted to cook my own food. Started by watching the cooking channels."

He used gyms regularly, so I could see him watching exercise programs. But cooking shows? I tried to imagine him watching one of those and couldn't do it.

He tossed his cup in a bin and placed his voting sheet in a box on a nearby table. "I need to leave to meet Michael. I'm glad you suggested this."

"Have fun. I'll see you tomorrow at Redwood Heights."

He left, and I looked around for familiar faces. It was hard to find anyone I knew in the now packed building. I spied Daniel towering above the crowd and started in his direction. People parted a bit, revealing Tina, Cindy, and Jerry chatting and tasting.

My eyes met Tina's. Her face reddened, and she turned away. I wondered if Deputy Sheriff Stanton had questioned her and the others yet.

I made my way to Daniel, Helen, and the kids.

"Miss Kelly, did you try the last chowder in the line? It's yummy good."

"Not yet, Tommy. I was about to go back. I'll go there first."

A familiar voice at my elbow said, "So glad you could make it, dear. What do you think of our little event?"

I turned to the Professor. "Overwhelmingly delicious. The combinations they've put together are over the top."

He could have walked out of one of the halls of an Ivy League school in his tweed jacket and matching cloth cap. Gertie and Mary were with him.

I looked around. "Where are Ivan and Rudy?"

"Making a second round," Mary said.

"Have you found Robert James yet?" I asked.

"We're not sure. We found some men who look like him. We have a few more pictures to take tomorrow morning," Mary said.

Gertie shifted her position on her cane. "Daniel's going to come over as soon as we have those photos to see if any of them are Robert James."

The Professor added, "A couple of them really look like the man in Gertie's photo. I think we have him."

"It'll be interesting to see if he has anything to add that'll further the investigation," I said.

I told them what I'd found that morning. The kids bombarded me with questions. A hidden passageway was a thing of intrigue. The Sentinels said they'd be over to the mansion in the afternoon for the event. After sampling the offerings from the few restaurants I hadn't tried yet, I voted for my favorite and drove home.

It had been a full day. Sleep came quickly.

In the morning I showered, slipped into my carriage house clothes, and fixed a light breakfast in my kitchen. I didn't have to be at the Heights for the Whale Frolic event until one, giving me plenty of time to do more searching. As I headed for my truck, I noticed the B & B was quiet. Apparently the Sentinels hadn't arrived yet and the kitchen was empty.

I pulled in next to the carriage house. Opening the door, I looked for a way to prop it open. Inside, on the floor next to the threshold, I found several wooden wedges. Someone before me had had the same idea. Probably one for the small door and a couple for the larger ones. I pushed the door back and slipped the device under the bottom edge, allowing the morning rays to brighten the gloomy interior.

As I did so, I noticed a pile of greasy rags next to the building. A gardener or a workman must have forgotten and left them there. I'd take care of them on my way out.

I hadn't walked through the whole building on my earlier visit and decided this was a good time to do so. Flipping on the lights, I began along the right-hand wall by pulling back dusty cloth covers and revealing chairs and couches. Miscellaneous gardening equipment leaned against the side of the building. Empty wooden barrels, the kinds I'd seen in wineries, were stacked on end along the back wall pyramid style, with six on the bottom and narrowing to two on top.

I found four more storage boxes and browsed their contents, hoping for more about Iris Reynolds and the lawsuit. The first one had black-and-white pictures—the paper as hard as thin cardboard. Each had two identical pictures on it. My grandmother had ones like these. She'd put one in a device called a stereoscope. When you looked through it, the photo came together as one picture. The other containers had books.

My attention was drawn to a glass cabinet hanging on the wall with a display of bridle bits. There were some very unusual pieces. One in particular had long silver sides with intricate engraving. These could be valuable.

A noise overhead made me look up. The rafters were high, and it was hard to see the upper portion of the building. I went over to my fanny pack and retrieved my flashlight. The beam revealed an intricately woven structure of branches and twigs on a crossbeam. I'd seen ones like it on the ranch and guessed it was a raven's nest.

As if to prove me right, a glossy black bird poked its head over the edge and eyed me.

"So, my dear raven, how are you getting in?"

The accommodating bird jumped onto a beam, ducked under the roof, and disappeared. I went outside and pushed through the low bushes along the edge of the building, peered up, and could barely make out a gap between the roof and the wall. Probably some dry rot there. I was becoming an expert on the stuff.

I felt something under my foot and looked to see what I'd stepped on. I found a quarter. There were a couple more coins next to it and a silver tab off of a soda can. Someone must've dropped them. I picked them up and put them in my pocket.

Back inside, I went over to the bit case, wondering if I should take the one I'd been admiring for safekeeping. I tried the door, and it opened easily. Stepping closer, I started to reach for it but stopped when my shoe scraped against something loose on the ground.

A couple more soda tabs were under foot. Next to them . . . a diamond ring. I snatched it up and studied it. It matched the description on the list of missing pieces. I looked up. It was directly under the raven's nest. I'd heard they were attracted to shiny items and had read a story about a raven stockpiling coins it stole from a vending machine. I'd noticed windows had been left open in many of the rooms on warm afternoons.

Maybe we had our thief! My heart raced. I'd noticed a tall metal ladder next to the fire extinguisher. I got it, put it under the nest, and looked up—a long way up. I hesitated. I'd learned from my days on the ranch, the higher the ladder, the more unstable. Even a sturdy ladder like this one could fall over. Then I thought of Stevie and Tina. If I was right, they'd be cleared of the thefts. I began climbing. The ladder wobbled a bit, but I kept going. Luckily, the nest was on the crossbeam and not all the way at the top of the building.

Standing on the last rung, I straightened up as tall as I could, holding the top of the ladder with both hands. I could barely see in, but I saw enough to have one answer to our problems. The hoard included a variety of bright objects, including jewelry and a few golf balls. The nest was too high for me to reach into it. I could only hope the bird wouldn't relocate anything until we'd had a chance to get the stolen goods back. I couldn't wait to tell Stanton . . . and Hensley. Stevie and Tina were in the clear.

A clattering near my right shoulder announced the raven's return. Before I could pull back, the raven was next to me, wings beating my head. I shrieked and covered my face with one arm, the other holding tight to the ladder.

"Stop! Get away!" I yelled and struck out at the bird.

My precarious perch wobbled, then toppled.

The ladder and I hurtled downward.

Chapter 20

I grabbed the ladder with both hands and threw my body to the right, attempting to twist it enough so the front of the ladder would fall on the stack of barrels. I was partly successful, as the front edge of the ladder hit the top two barrels, sending them cascading end over end and smashing into the back wall. The ladder bumped down to the next row of three and settled at an angle . . . tilting precariously.

My heart raced, but I froze in place, waiting to see if there would be any further shifting. After a minute that seemed like an eternity, I moved my right foot down a rung and stopped. No movement. Two more steps and the ladder slid down a few inches. I clung to the sides, waited a few seconds, and then continued down even more slowly than before. Making it to the bottom, with a few more scares, I sagged against the ladder, trembling from the adrenaline racing through my body.

That was too close for comfort. I felt like kissing the ground.

I wiped my sweaty palms on my jeans and walked over to view the damage. The barrels had gouged a couple of very large holes in the wall. I peered into one, but the meager light in the room couldn't penetrate the pitch black. I searched for my flashlight and found it where I'd dropped it during the fall. I turned it on and looked through the opening of one of the broken areas.

I gasped.

I'd expected to see a retaining wall at the back of the cave. Instead, my light showed stacks of steamer trunks and wooden traveling boxes in various sizes, and—I blinked—an old-fashioned horse carriage. Redwood Heights was full of surprises.

One of the holes was almost big enough for me to squeeze through if I pulled the shattered boards off. I removed the canvas cover off of the furniture and used the material to protect my hands as I took off the loose pieces of wood. If I was careful, I'd be able to get through without snagging myself on the jagged edges.

I crawled through the opening and flashed my light around. A blanket of undisturbed dust covered everything. I examined the first trunk. It was wooden and decorated with brass stars dulled with age. I aimed my light at a large tag with bold, black writing. Unfortunately, the swirling penmanship on the yellowed tag was impossible to read.

I pulled on the metal handle and flipped the heavy lid back. My light flickered and went out, reminding me of how little light was making it into the room. Darn. The fall must've loosened something. I shook it and was relieved when it came back to life.

Ruffles, lace, and beads adorning the bodice of a midnight blue dress showed in the light. I turned the beam to the edge of the box. There was enough room for me to run my hand down the side and flip through the contents. Silk, cotton, and wool garments in the colors of the rainbow with a few plaids thrown in. A lady's wardrobe.

The next chest, smaller in size, was made of dark wood and had decorative brass-covered edges. On one side lay a stack of framed photographs, the top picture displaying a young woman in a ball gown, her dark hair piled high in an intricate hairdo. Examining a few more photos, I discovered the same woman in all of them. In one she was on the arm of Mr. Brandon. The glass had been cracked. The other side of the trunk held intricate hand-embroidered flowers flowing across the back of a pair of black gloves. Underneath them were more gloves and some delicate fans.

That completed the contents of the trunk. Turning, I moved the light around the room. The carriage loomed out of the darkness, bits of the ornate gold design adorning the door reflecting back at me. The horses on the Brandon crest conveyed pride and strength, in spite of being cracked and peeling.

Why was it here? How long had it been sealed away? The door to the carriage beckoned. I turned the light on the floor to see if there was anything in the way and saw only a dust carpet between myself and the carriage.

Walking toward it, I ran the light over the aged surface, revealing tarnished brass fixtures and the dark eyes of the empty carriage windows. I reached for the door handle and hesitated. Deciding to look inside first, I climbed on the step of the carriage, held on to the metal grip mounted beside the door, and stood on my toes, my eyes barely above the window rim. I lifted the light above my head and aimed it inside.

I screamed, jerked the flashlight's beam away from the hideous sight, and jumped back off the step. My light went out again.

Frantically, I shook it, while the last image did a macabre dance in my mind. Dark holes where eyes had once been; sparkling jewels adorning bones. I shook the light harder.

The light revived, illuminating the trunks and boxes. I moved the light slowly back around to the carriage and its occupant. I had glimpsed fine black lace and pieces of faded red satin. A hat with the remains of a sweeping feather had slipped onto the figure's shoulder.

Reminding myself whoever was inside was far, far past doing me any harm, I took a deep breath, pushed my willpower into full gear, and opted for the door this time. Who was this person? I cautiously moved the lever. The door screeched at my uninvited presence. The figure reposed on a worn leather seat. Remnants of material clung to the skeleton. An intricate necklace rested on the bodice of what had once been a dress. Earrings had fallen on the cushion.

One of the woman's hands rested in her lap, the bony fingers holding a yellowed envelope. The other rested on a small wooden box and a tattered tassel lying across its top. An aged leather portfolio rested at her feet, the Brandon crest faintly visible.

The entombed carriage and its occupant needed to be reported. I eyed the case, the box, and the brittle-looking paper. Deputy Sheriff Stanton had told me not to investigate on my own. But this was different. It had probably been more than a century since this woman had last enjoyed fresh air. The hatpin had gone missing, and I didn't want to take a chance on anything else disappearing.

A rain of dust softly fell on my hair and shoulders as I leaned into the cab. Shreds of a voluminous red skirt had small, tattered cloth-covered triangles poking out from under the hem. Shoes she no longer needed. A fixed yellow-toothed grin greeted the first visitor in decades. I pulled the portfolio out and put it on the floor.

I'm closer than I want to be, but I'm not close enough.

I put my knees on the carriage floor, grabbed the cushion across from the skeleton, and crawled in. I crouched down in the small foot space within inches of the gruesome occupant.

Get the envelope. Get the box. Get out of there.

Putting my thumb and forefinger on the aged envelope, I tugged gently. It moved slightly. I pulled again. Stuck. The dust was beginning to work its way up my nose; drops of perspiration trickled down my face.

The empty sockets seem to be turned toward me. How dare I intrude? What was I doing in her carriage?

I yanked and the skeletal hand parted from the rest of the body and clattered to the carriage floor in a rain of small bones. Falling back, I fought a wave of nausea. I looked over my shoulder at the opening in the wall, streaming with light, leading back into the carriage house, and willed myself to be calm. Placing the envelope in my fleece pocket, I turned back to get the box.

Gingerly, I reached out and began to work it away from the other hand. An object fell off of one of the bony fingers. A cameo ring with an ivory silhouette of a woman's face slowly rolled to a stop next to my foot.

I had the box; the hand rested on the seat. I quickly backed out of the carriage.

"No offense, I just don't want to overstay my visit," I muttered to the silent hostess.

My right hand fit through the handle of the case, and I pushed it up onto my arm. Holding the box under my arm with my left hand, my flashlight in my right, I struggled forward with my awkward load. I was determined to make only one trip at if at all possible.

When I reached the opening, I put down the case, leaned through, and placed the box on the floor on the other side. Doing the same with the case, I then crawled through and into the main room of the carriage house.

The openness of the large room was welcome after the close quarters with the skeleton. I took a deep breath and slipped my flashlight into my pocket. I pulled out the envelope. The back had a cracked, purple wax seal with the Brandon emblem. I carefully removed a piece of brittle parchment paper, discolored with age. Placing the envelope on top of the leather case, I unfolded the single stiff sheet.

> *Dear Violet,*
> *I promised to keep you in finery always. I am a man of my*
> *word. May you forever rest in peace in your satin and jewels.*
> *Reginald Brandon*

The missing Mrs. Brandon. It wasn't a myth. I'd always believed the docents of old mansions often embellished the family history with a few additional skeletons in the closet and thought maybe Redwood Heights had been no different. This time the story was true. I was faced with another murder, though, one belonging in the annals of history, not the front page of the daily paper.

I put the letter back in the envelope and sat on the floor next to the leather case and the box, which I suspected was a writing slope. My family had one of these at the ranch. My great-grandfather used it to keep meticulous records. The angled surface formed a comfortable writing area for long periods of work. Using the cloth cover that had helped me remove the boards, I dusted the top of it and found a detailed pattern of mother-of-pearl inlay. The front was smashed where a lock would've been.

I opened it, reached inside, and pulled out a stack of folded papers held together by a faded blue ribbon. I untied the bow, opened the packet, and began reading the top letter.

It quickly became clear to me Mrs. Brandon had a lover. My face heated as I read the passionate words he'd written. I didn't want to intrude on their long-ago intimacy and skimmed through the rest of the letter. I stopped at the last paragraph.

The flowing hand had written, "We must think of a way to get rid of him so we can be together always, Violet. Think, as I will, and together we'll devise a plan."

I scanned the rest of the letters, then turned to the leather case, unbuckling the tarnished metal clasp, bending back the cracked brown leather, and found several more packets of letters. I went through them, traveling back in time. They revealed that the couple planned on killing Brandon and living together at the estate. Then she got pregnant. She hadn't slept with her husband for months—he'd know the baby wasn't his. They put their plans on hold while she traveled back east to have the child, leaving before Brandon could detect she was pregnant. After the birth, she'd planned to leave the child with relatives and return so they could finish their business with Brandon.

I knew enough of the history to know she had indeed returned after an extended visit to New York. That part of their plan had come to pass. Obviously, from the body in the carriage, the rest of it didn't. It also meant there was a good likelihood she'd had a baby—if so, it meant there'd been someone who thought they had the right to inherit the mansion.

I checked my watch and put the papers away. I needed to get back to the inn and change for the whale event . . . and call the police. Standing, I noticed the door had closed at some point. I'd been so engrossed I hadn't been aware of it. The wedge must have come undone.

Then I smelled it.

Smoke.

Chapter 21

I looked around. Wisps of smoke were coming from under the door. I ran over and tried to open it, yanking the door back and forth.

It didn't budge. Something had to be holding it in place.

Getting down on my knees, I looked under the bottom. I could see an object there. Had the wedge accidentally gotten turned around and was holding the door shut? And what was burning? Had the rags spontaneously combusted?

The smoke was getting thicker. I called 911, my fingers shaking as I dialed, but Redwood Cove only had a volunteer fire department—it would take them a while to get there. They answered, and I told them the situation and where I was. I pulled the alarm on the wall but didn't know how far the sound would carry. The windows were high and small. I could get up there with the ladder, but I wasn't sure I'd be able to get through them.

There was a fire extinguisher next to the alarm. Grabbing it, I sprayed under the door. The smoke continued to pour in. I needed to get out of there, which meant unjamming the door.

I knelt down again and tried to reach the item with my fingers, scraping the skin on the back of my hands. The distance between the bottom of the door and floor was almost enough for me to reach the object, but not quite. I needed something to push back whatever was holding the door in place. Smoke was filling the room. I coughed and coughed again. Then I remembered the old photographs I'd seen earlier—like cardboard, thin and stiff. They might work.

I raced to the box and grabbed a handful of them. Putting two of them together, I pushed them under the door and felt the object move. There was room for a third photo, so I added it, making my tool stronger. The resistance suddenly gave way as the pictures slid through under the door. I'd done it! Whatever had been jammed under the door was dislodged.

I jumped up, turned the handle, and stumbled outside, tripping on smoldering rags. I managed to keep my balance and rushed back inside for the fire extinguisher. I coated the rags with foam, put the fire extinguisher down, and sank to my knees. Shifting to a sitting position, I closed my eyes.

They flew open as I felt myself showered in dog kisses. Two ecstatic beagles beamed at me. Stevie and Deputy Sheriff Stanton ran toward me.

Stanton knelt beside me. "Ms. Jackson, are you okay?"

"I think so," I croaked, my throat raw from the smoke. I hadn't had time to evaluate my condition yet.

The rags had begun to smoke again. "There's a fire extinguisher beside the door," I wheezed.

He stood, got it, and smothered the pieces of cloth completely. Sirens approached.

Stevie sat down next to me and put his arm around my shoulders. "I'm glad you're okay." He sat there, caring and supportive.

"What made you come here?" I asked.

"Deputy Sheriff Stanton and I were talking when Jack and Jill went ballistic, howling and lunging against their leashes. They were clearly trying to tell us something. We looked in the direction they were pulling and saw the smoke. We ran toward it and heard the alarm as we approached. The dogs probably heard it when we couldn't and smelled the smoke as well."

I gave the dogs a hug. Their fast-moving tails would have fanned the fire, so I was glad it was out.

A team of firemen arrived.

"I think we have it under control," Deputy Stanton told them. "I'd like you to check the rags and inside the carriage house to make sure."

As my calm returned, I realized the rags weren't where I'd seen them earlier. They'd been at the side of the building before, not in front of the door. I got up and looked around where I'd dislodged what had jammed the door. I found the triangular piece of wood I'd used earlier. It had indeed been turned around to hold the door closed.

I was standing near Deputy Stanton. One of the firemen came up to him with some of the rags in his hand.

"Deputy Stanton, there's a smell of gasoline and a match. This was deliberately set. We're lucky the material was damp from the fog this morning."

The wedge secured the door, locking me in.

The rags had been moved and lit on fire.

Someone had tried to kill me.

A flash of fear followed.

Deputy Sheriff Stanton walked over to me. "I'm guessing you heard."

I nodded. "I'd wedged the door open when I got here. I thought somehow it had gotten loose and turned around. It appears it had some help."

"Tell me what's been going on."

There was a lot to tell. I handed him the diamond ring and explained about the raven, the fall, and the walled-off room.

I gave him the details of what I'd found. "I think you have two mysteries solved, Deputy Sheriff . . . what happened to the missing Mrs. Brandon and the identity of the jewel thief."

"You've had a busy morning, Ms. Jackson."

"Let me show you the items I removed from the carriage."

We went inside. The firemen had opened the large carriage house doors, but a haze of smoke still filled the air. It would take a while for it to clear.

Handing him the letter, I pointed to the leather case and the box. "These will have the information I shared with you."

He nodded and then shined his light into the newly discovered room, the tomb of Mrs. Brandon, and gave a low whistle. "This could be quite a find for our local history buffs, depending on what Mr. Corrigan wants to do with the stuff."

"I'll ask him what he plans to do with it."

"Thanks." Deputy Sheriff Stanton closed the notepad he'd been writing in and looked at me. "Don't say anything about the skeleton and the fire for now. I want to question people first."

"Okay. What about the raven and the jewelry? Can I tell Stevie?"

"That's fine. It'll take some of the tension away, and that's a good thing." He smiled. "And now Gertie'll get off my back for questioning Stevie. That'll be a *very* good thing."

I went back outside. Stevie and the beagles were seated where they'd found me. "Stevie, I know who, or rather what, stole the jewelry." Excitement lit his face. "Who did it?" I told him what I'd found. "The police can't charge you or anyone else now. They have to go after a bird!" He gave me a hug. "Thank you so much. What an incredible relief!"

I returned to Deputy Sheriff Stanton. "I'd like to go and get ready for the event this afternoon."

"Ms. Jackson,"—he looked at me—"it appears someone made an attempt on your life. You need to be very careful."

"I understand."

"If you think of anything new, even if it seems trivial, call me."

"I will," I promised.

"Okay. You can go."

I bid Stevie good-bye, got in the truck, and drove back to Redwood Cove B & B. The jewelry thefts were solved. A murder was solved, albeit an old one. And an attack had been made on my life. Quite a morning indeed.

The inn had a second door in back, which we rarely used. Knowing I reeked of smoke, I decided to go in that way to avoid awkward questions. I unlocked it and entered the hallway. A washer and dryer were on my right, followed by the linen closet, and then the conference room. I walked farther down the hall and to my room.

I showered, put on clean jeans and a T-shirt, and then took my smoke- and dust-tainted clothes to the washer and got them started. Walking back, I checked the conference room. There were no Sentinels, but there was a picture with a sign underneath it and large red letters stating, "Robert James!!!" with Oceanside Lodge and Suites underneath it.

I studied the picture, thinking it looked like the billionaire Sylvia showed me named Robert Johnson. I couldn't be sure, as I'd only seen the photograph once. Maybe it was his doppelgänger. Or maybe he was using an alias to avoid people like Sylvia. It didn't matter if it was him or not. They'd found the man the police wanted to question. It was a long shot he had anything to do with Sylvia's murder, especially since he wasn't staying there that day, but it was one more step in the investigation.

I went to the office and took a stack of brochures out of the desk drawer and studied them. Corrigan had involved me in the renovation, and I'd suggested creating names and themes for the rooms. It had been a fun project, and seeing the pictures and descriptions showed it had come to fruition. I was excited about working with the public for the first time as manager of Redwood Cove B & B and wanted to put the events of the morning to the back of my mind so I could enjoy the experience.

Going through the multipurpose room on my way out, I saw the kids hard at work on their projects at the table. Fred seemed to be in the same position I'd seen him in earlier—touching both Tommy and Allie. This time he deigned to acknowledge me by lifting his head and wagging his tail. I think I was moving up on his "like" list.

"How's the work going?" I asked.

"We're making presentation boards." Tommy jumped up. He grabbed a large piece of folded cardboard, opened it, and put it on the table, revealing a trifold with a wonderful, elaborate display. He did the same with a second one. The kids had glued pictures of whales and placed ocean-themed stickers on the boards.

Allie picked up a miniature blue-and-white lighthouse, peeled the backing off, and placed it in the upper right-hand corner of one. "I'm learning a lot of new things. I never knew things like this existed," she said as she picked up some pearlescent seashells stickers.

Tommy chose a glittering starfish from the pile in front of him. "Mom got them for us. They're really neat." He held up a replica of a piling from a wharf, real twine wrapped around it, with a seagull perched on top.

Helen came over and stood beside me. "Our local crafts store has a large scrapbooking section. I thought the kids would have fun with them."

"We are!" exclaimed Allie. "Thank you so much."

Helen turned to me. "Did you hear the good news? The Sentinels found Robert James."

"I didn't hear it, but I saw it in big letters with lots of exclamation marks."

"They're an amazing group. When they put their minds to something, it gets done."

As I drove to the mansion, thoughts of the morning's attack pushed their way into my mind, in spite of my efforts to deny them access. Who had tried to kill me? What had I done? What did they think I knew?

I was asking myself the same questions I'd asked to find Sylvia's murderer . . . only this time the questions were about me.

Chapter 22

I parked in front of the mansion, knowing visitors would be using the back lot, and walked to the kitchen to see what I could do to help. When I got there, Tina and Cindy were deep in concentration garnishing appetizers with sprigs of parsley. Lily stood at one of the counters, placing an assortment of crackers on a tray.

I looked forward to telling her about my find when I could. "Lily, where's a good place for me to put my purse?"

"Look in the bottom left-hand cabinet over there." She nodded in the direction of the wall adjacent to the washroom.

"Thanks."

Opening it, I added my purse to the others stored there by the staff. I went back and stood next to Lily, admiring her dress. It was a white, brown, and pale green plaid. Ruffles adorned the shoulders and the hem. Her hat sported a long, delicate feather.

"That's quite an ensemble, Lily."

Lily made a complete turn, showing me the entire garment. "It's a vintage madras day dress, probably from the eighteen sixties. Resorts International gives me a budget for my outfits and, using the Internet, I've been able to find wonderful pieces."

Hensley walked in and surveyed the room. Did she know anything about the man Sylvia had said was Robert Johnson?

Seizing the opportunity, I said, "Margaret, the Sentinels have found Robert James. However, the photo of him looks like one Sylvia showed me. She'd said it was billionaire Robert Johnson. Do you know anyone by that name?"

"It sounds familiar. I'm sure I know something about him." She frowned, then shook her head. "It's not coming to me right now, but it will."

Tina and Cindy straightened up, their edible creations completed, then gave each other a high five.

I walked over. "These are beautiful. I never in a thousand years would've thought raw cooking could create masterpieces like these."

"And," Cindy said, "it's not just about their appearance. Wait until you taste them."

"I'm looking forward to it." Had Deputy Stanton told her about the raven?

"Do you know we found the jewel thief?"

"No!" Tina exclaimed. "Who is it?"

I could understand why it wasn't a priority of the deputy's, and so I explained about the raven. I could see Hensley out of the corner of my eye. She didn't look surprised. I guessed Deputy Stanton had returned the diamond ring, along with an explanation. It would've been nice of her to say something to Tina, but nice didn't seem to be part of her makeup.

"Wow! Thanks. That's been a cloud over my head. I can enjoy today even more."

"I'm glad it's resolved, too."

"Kelly." Tina hesitated. "We'd like to talk to you for a few minutes before the event begins."

"Sure, if there's time. Let me check what's happening." I wondered what they wanted to talk about.

Lily sailed by me, full skirt billowing and ostrich feather quivering. A platter of crackers appeared ready to go, so I took it with me. Had Deputy Stanton talked to them yet about the alibis? Tina hadn't appeared upset.

The side porch was enclosed in glass. Two long rectangular tables decorated with beautiful bouquets of flowers were on each side of the room. Appetizers rested on the tables, which had been pulled away from the wall so people would have room to move on both sides. The wine stations were set up at the back of the porch.

Phil's whistling filled the room. He nodded a hello and did a couple of Greek dance steps. He knew I enjoyed line dancing, and he was a master dancer. Phil whirled and spun, his feet tapping out intricate steps. He gave a final bow with a flourish of his arms.

I clapped. "It's always such a delight to watch you, Phil."

Andy, on the other side of the room, waved as he perused his cheese trays, making minute changes here and there. I joined him.

"Kelly, hi. I have some excellent cheeses for you today, including a Huntsman and a smoked Gouda. I encourage you to try them all."

"I don't need any encouragement. You've taught me a lot about the exquisite taste of artisan cheeses."

Areas at the ends of the food tables remained clear. Daniel was putting out brochures in one of those spots.

Hensley swept into the room. "Kelly, I'd like you to set up on the end of that table over there." She pointed to one opposite Daniel. "I'm putting out information on Redwood Heights and Resorts International on the other ends."

I spread my brochures out, a thrill running through me as I looked at them. My new job. My new life. My new home.

I looked at the tray of appetizers nearest me. Cards listing the ingredients rested in holders in front of them. Clever. That would entice people to ask questions and forewarn anyone with food sensitivities. I checked my watch. We had twenty minutes before the doors opened.

I went back to the kitchen to find out what Tina and Cindy wanted to talk to me about. When I got there, I found Jerry had joined them.

"Let's go in the washroom," Tina said.

We went back to the area where I'd found the passageway yesterday. I was burning with curiosity to hear what they had to say.

"Deputy Sheriff Stanton questioned us," Tina said. "He—"

I interrupted her. "I'm sorry, Tina. I had to tell him when I realized the alibi Jerry and Cindy had was no longer valid."

"We completely understand and want to thank you for talking to Deputy Sheriff Stanton about protecting Jerry's reputation," Cindy said. "We really appreciate it."

"The good news is he was able to do it," Tina said.

Jerry nodded. "We actually do have alibis. They just aren't quite what we told the police." He didn't look at me as he made this admission.

Cindy chimed in. "I ran into him at the school when I was picking up supplies for today. It was after Tina texted me."

Jerry picked up the line of the conversation. "I had made arrangements to meet the owners and used an alias." His face reddened. "When I heard the police were asking questions, I asked Cindy to cover for me."

"We were protecting the Meat King," Cindy said.

The girls giggled.

"I'm not leaving meat cooking behind," he hastened to add, "but when I began to learn more about raw food cooking, I was fascinated by what can be done and wanted to learn more."

"We had lunch together and then went to the class," Cindy said.

"After we complete our courses and get our certificates, Jerry's going to help us start a small business with a café and catering." Tina's eyes glowed. "He'll be a silent partner."

"I'll be more than silent, I'll be an invisible partner." We all laughed. "At least in the beginning. We'll see where it goes."

"That's great news. Congratulations to all three of you."

"We've been having fun. We work well together," Jerry said, "which isn't always the case in the cooking world."

I glanced at my watch. "There are only a few more minutes before the event begins."

Jerry said, "It's time for me to exit out the back and enter in the front." He gave a wave and was gone.

I went to the porch and took my station. The doors opened and people flooded in. Corrigan came over and stood next to me, greeting guests. He smiled at them, but the smile didn't reach his eyes.

He turned to me. "Deputy Sheriff Stanton told Scott and me what happened. Are you okay?"

"Yes. I'm fine. Just a few scraped fingers."

"I want to talk to you as soon as this is done. I don't want you to leave the building for any reason."

His serious tone brought back the specter of the morning's attempt on my life. "All right."

"We'll talk about what I've got planned."

The next couple of hours were a whirlwind of activity. Time flew by. The crowds didn't come and go as Corrigan had said. They came and stayed. New people kept arriving; the throng never diminished.

I stepped in several times to help Andy and Phil pour wine, directing questions about the cheese and wine to them. Tina and Cindy replaced trays of food and glasses. Scott hovered by the Resorts International information. Corrigan split his time at the four places advertising his company and helping as needed.

Judging by the buzz around the raw food appetizers, they were a hit. About half a dozen people peppered Cindy and Tina with questions and requests for recipes. Their faces shined, their gestures animated. Who knew raw food could be so much fun?

Jerry stood off to the side. He was an astute businessman. You didn't get a title like Meat King offered to you on a platter. He'd worked for it. Jerry would figure out a way to bring the two styles of cooking together.

The Silver Sentinels made their way through the crowd, which wasn't hard with Ivan at the bow, breaking through the waves of people.

Mary's sweet perfume enveloped me as she picked up a brochure. "Oh, honey, these are gorgeous."

Gertie opened one and scanned the pictures. "Smart idea, the themed rooms. People will find favorites and want to come back to their special one."

The Professor pointed to one of the pictures. "What good taste you have, Kelly. I'd want to stay in this room." The picture showed a large brown leather chair pulled up next to a fireplace, a stack of magazines on the table next to it, and a bookcase filled with books.

Rudy looked at the pamphlet. "That looks like your house, Professor."

"Yes, indeed it does. Must be why I like it."

I handed a brochure to an interested passerby. "Please let me know if you have any questions."

The Professor closed the pamphlet and placed it on the table. "My dear, we're having an impromptu dinner in the conference room this evening. Now that we've located Robert James, we want to assess where we are and decide on next steps. We'd love to have you join us."

Information sharing, planning next steps, and dinner with friends sounded perfect—especially after the day I'd had. "Good idea, Professor. I'd love to."

"Fine, then. We'll see you later." With a nod, the Professor and the rest of the group wandered off.

I glanced around a couple times during the busy afternoon. Hensley looked every inch the charming hostess. Andy blew air kisses as he raved about his cheese, his passion showing. Phil was too far away for me to see his eyes, but I'm sure they were twinkling as he talked about merlots, zinfandels, and chardonnays.

The event ended at three thirty, and Andy and Phil began to put away wineglasses. The crowd started to thin. Some women examined the ruffles on Lily's dress, and a few stragglers at the appetizer table were taking notes as Cindy and Tina talked. Scott was picking up brochures. I didn't see Hensley.

Corrigan came over to me. "Let's meet in the housekeeping office. We won't be disturbed there."

I'd already picked up a couple of platters. "Okay. I'll rinse these off and be right there."

As I cleaned the dishes, I thought about what the day had brought to the investigation. Jerry and Cindy were off the suspect list. Would Robert James have an alibi and shorten the list that much more? Since I'd solved the jewel thefts, Tina and Stevie were in the clear on that. And someone apparently wanted me dead, and I had no idea why. Disturbing, to say the least. I dried my hands and joined my boss.

The office was brightly lit, which made up for the lack of windows. I sat in front of the desk.

Corrigan picked up a pencil and began rolling it between his fingers. "Kelly, an attempt was made on your life. Until we catch whoever did it, I don't want you going places on your own."

I frowned. "But that really limits me, Michael. I should be okay in public places. I promise not to go anywhere isolated."

"I understand, but your safety comes first. I've arranged for Detective Rodriguez to stay at Redwood Cove B and B tonight. Helen's prepared a room for him and one for you, too."

"But I have a room."

"It's too isolated, and all that glass is easy to break. You'll have a room next to the detective."

"But what about errands and putting the final touches on the inn?"

"Daniel, Scott, and I will make ourselves as available as possible to accompany you." Corrigan smiled. "And no more 'buts,' please."

I sighed. "What we need to do is figure out who's behind all of this. At least we made some progress today. The Silver Sentinels found Robert James. I saw his photo pinned up with where he's staying written beneath it."

"Good news, though I doubt he has anything to do with any of this."

"I agree. Funny thing, he looks just like the man Sylvia said was Robert Johnson, a billionaire."

The pencil snapped. Corrigan abruptly stood and tossed the pencil on the desk. His hands balled into fists, knuckles white. "I want to see that picture. Now." He headed for the door.

Startled, I hurried after him, almost having to run to keep up. What had enraged my hard-to-ruffle boss?

Chapter 23

Corrigan didn't say a word as we drove to the inn. Anger emanated from him. He parked, got out, slammed the door, and headed for the back door.

I thought about Tommy and Allie. "Michael." I caught up with him and put my hand on his arm. "I can tell you're really upset. Others will know it, too. The kids were working on school projects in the main room earlier today. Let's go in the other door."

He took a deep breath, and his features relaxed a bit. "Good idea."

I unlocked the back door I'd used earlier in the day, and we entered.

"If the man in the photo is Robert Johnson, that's going to bring an unpleasant past into the present," he said.

In the conference room, he went over to the picture and stared... and stared... and stared. He took out his phone. "Deputy Sheriff Stanton, the man you know as Robert James is really Robert Johnson, my ex-partner, and he was trespassing when he stayed at Redwood Heights."

His former partner? Trespassing? There must be some serious history between the two with all that anger.

"Yes, I can come over now." Ending the call, he turned to me. "He has Johnson at the mansion in the interview room. Let's go. I want you staying with me until we have things sorted out for the evening."

The drive back was fast, but his large figure charging for the interview room seemed faster.

Corrigan made a beeline for the slim, dark-haired man standing next to Deputy Sheriff Stanton. "I told you to never set foot on any of my properties again. How dare you—"

I thought he might grab him by the front of his shirt. Apparently Deputy Stanton felt the same way, as he stepped in front of Corrigan.

"Hello, Michael," the man said, his voice calm, clearly not disturbed by Michael's entrance. "It seems the years haven't cooled your anger."

"Mr. Corrigan," Deputy Stanton said, "I asked you to join us with the thought you might have something to add to the questioning. If that's not the case, I'll need you to leave." He turned to the other man. "Mr. Johnson, take a seat."

Robert Johnson went around the table and sat facing Stanton.

Michael didn't move immediately. When he did, he placed himself where he could stare at his ex-partner. I decided to sit on the periphery of the group and chose a place at the end of the table.

Deputy Stanton sat back. "There are clearly strong feelings between the two of you. What's that about?"

Robert Johnson glanced at Michael then started. "Michael Corrigan and I met at Harvard. We did a few projects together, initially, just for the fun of it, to see what we could do. We found we worked well as a team, and when we graduated, we went into business together."

Stanton had his pen and notebook out. "How long did that last?"

"We were together for almost eight years and did extremely well financially. That allowed us to begin to explore special areas of interest. I became fascinated with new technology and how it could be implemented in a resort site." He looked at his ex-partner. "Your turn."

"While Robert went high-tech, I became interested in preserving our country's heritage. I began to explore ways to modernize buildings that would allow them to keep their uniqueness and be enjoyed by people today." He stopped. A couple of minutes passed.

Robert Johnson broke the silence. "People such as foreign dignitaries, rock stars, politicians, and the very wealthy are a diverse group with one thing in common—a need for safety. I wanted to provide them with a place where they could relax without being in the shadows of their bodyguards. A resort where they didn't need to worry about their kids being kidnapped. The geographical placement of a place like that is critical in terms of security." He quit talking.

Deputy Stanton tapped his pen on his notebook. "Go on."

"We bought a piece of property whose location was perfect for my dream. It was also a renowned vacation destination for the rich and famous in the late eighteen hundreds." He stopped for a moment. "I ended up with the land for a number of reasons. It was impossible to incorporate the sensitive security equipment needed for my plan and use the original buildings."

"What he's neglecting to tell you is the property in question is where my parents were married," Michael said through gritted teeth. "I'd made a promise to restore it in their memory."

"They were gone, Michael. What difference did it make?"

"You didn't get it then, and you still don't. Some places are about people's lives and the memories they bring. This place was one of those." His voice increased in volume. "I went to take one last look at the building, not realizing your wrecking crew had already started demolishing it." His voice seethed. "It wasn't just a building, it was a piece of history—personal and public—something that couldn't be replaced. What I saw ripped me apart."

That was probably what he'd like to do to his ex-partner.

"The people I help have a right to live a normal life whenever they can." Johnson's cool demeanor was gone. "They count, too."

"We could've found you another place," Corrigan countered.

Their voices escalated.

"Michael, I'd been looking for a long time. It was my dream, and I saw a chance to make it happen."

There it was. This was what caused the rift. Opposing ideologies colliding and crushing a close friendship.

Michael stood and leaned toward Johnson. "You could've—"

Deputy Sheriff Stanton cut in. "Gentlemen, that covers the past. What brought you here, Mr. Johnson?"

Corrigan sat.

"A while back, I heard this place was for sale. After doing some research, I felt it would be perfect for one of my resorts, only I needed more land than what came with this property. My staff found that most of the adjacent land was owned by the Bernal Corporation in San Francisco. I got in touch with the CEO. He wasn't interested in selling . . . had some grand plan to build a posh community." Johnson shook his head. "The guy's a novice. It turns out he's never built anything like that before. After I pointed out a few things he'd have to do and how much it would cost, he was more amenable to selling."

Corrigan interrupted him. "You know I won't sell anything to you."

Johnson didn't acknowledge him. "However, there were a couple more lots needed to make the deal work, so I didn't purchase it. You stepped in and bought the place. When you put it on the market, the CEO contacted me to let me know he'd acquired the additional properties." He stared at Michael. "Yes, I know you won't sell me anything. That's why I asked this guy to buy it and then transfer it to me."

"At one time, you had integrity. It seems that's gone now."

Johnson looked away.

Deputy Stanton said, "Did you meet Sylvia Porter during your stay here?"

"No. I kept to myself as much as possible. I didn't want to be recognized."

"Mrs. Porter's dead," Deputy Stanton said. "Murdered."

Johnson looked at the deputy. "Do you think I had something to do with her death?"

"We're questioning anyone staying here at the time Mrs. Porter was here. Where were you Thursday between the hours of eleven thirty and twelve forty-five?"

"Doing paperwork for the sale."

"Was anyone with you?"

"No."

"What about this morning between ten and ten thirty?"

Interesting. Stanton was looking for a connection between the attack on me and the murder.

"More of the same. The deal was supposed to close tomorrow."

"Why did you trespass?"

"I knew Michael was at a conference. It was an opportunity for me to see the place. I had a staff member book a room and cancel at the last minute so I could step in."

Michael spoke. "Robert, it's possible that a multimillion-dollar deal like this one could be the impetus for someone to commit murder. It's certainly happened to others in similar situations. One of my employees lost her life. Who had a stake in this sale?"

"The CEO, Mark Benton, and his sister. He'd get the money. She'd been wanting to try her hand at running a hotel or B and B. I cut them a good deal on the mansion. I'd still own it, but they had a long-term lease for a song. I wanted the property behind it."

"Is there anything you can think of that might connect what you were doing to Mrs. Porter being killed if the deal didn't go through?" Stanton asked.

"Not really. As I said, I had to talk the CEO into selling. He'd just go back to his original plans. His sister wouldn't have any trouble finding another place to run. People burn out in that business."

Deputy Stanton closed his notebook. "If you think of anything, let me know . . . and keep us informed as to your whereabouts."

Johnson stood and began pacing. From his tasseled cordovan leather loafers to the soft luster of the pale yellow blazer, the high-tech resort owner reflected the clientele he catered to. He stopped in front of Corrigan.

"Michael, you don't want the place, and I do. I want it very badly. The mansion would stay intact. If you sell it to someone else, it might end up being sold again and destroyed, like what almost happened before you purchased it. Reconsider."

"Not now. Not ever." Corrigan put his hands on the table, fingers spread. "No deal, Robert."

"If it means anything, Michael, I regret the decision I made about using the property you cared so much about for my first resort."

Corrigan stood and strode out of the room, with me right behind him.

He stopped in the hallway. "Do you know who's at your inn right now?"

"The Silver Sentinels invited me to join them there for dinner. They should be there by now."

"Good. I'll follow you back to the inn, and Detective Rodriguez will join you later."

My keys were in my purse, which was still in the cupboard. We'd left so suddenly earlier, I hadn't retrieved it. "I need to get my things from the kitchen."

Corrigan glanced down the hallway. The kitchen door was in sight. "Okay. I'll wait here for you." He pulled out his phone.

Retrieving my purse, I decided to peek into the passageway and see if the police were there and whether or not they'd discovered anything. The door to the hidden hallway was closed. I opened it and saw no sign of anyone. They must've finished for now.

I started to close the door. A low moan came from the dark. I froze. A burst of adrenaline shot through me and the hair on my arms stood up. I felt rooted in place. Had my ghostly acquaintances of yesterday not been a figment of my imagination? If I looked, would I see a spectral figure?

Another moan. My breath came fast. Trembling, I opened my purse and took out my flashlight. I paused before turning it on. What was I going to see? I clenched my teeth and turned on the light.

I moved the beam slowly up the passageway. A few feet in, my light fell on the bottoms of a pair of shoes. I stepped into the hallway and cast the light on the prone figure.

Margaret Hensley . . . blood trickling down the side of her face.

Chapter 24

I knelt beside her and touched her arm. Her skin felt clammy. "Margaret, can you hear me?"

She moaned again but didn't open her eyes.

I briefly examined her wound—it didn't look deep, but there was a lot of blood. I got up, stepped out of the passageway, and punched in 911 on my phone while yelling, "Michael!"

He came running into the room. I gestured with my hand toward the passageway and handed him my flashlight as I put my phone to my ear.

"Nine-one-one. What's your emergency?"

"A woman's been injured. She has a gash on the side of her head and is unconscious. She may have been attacked."

"What is your location?"

"Redwood Heights Mansion in Redwood Cove. The address is one hundred Redwood Drive. We're in the back of the building."

"Will you be able to be reached at this number?"

"Yes."

"An ambulance and the police will be dispatched."

Ending the call, I speed-dialed Scott.

"Hi, Kelly, what's up?"

"Margaret's been hurt. I don't think it was an accident. We're at the entrance to the passageway."

"I'm on my way. The detectives said they'd be working in the interview room. I'll swing by and get them."

I scanned the walls for another flashlight. Extras were usually kept easily accessible in case of power failures. I found one by the door to the kitchen. It was large and could also be used as a lantern.

Joining Corrigan, I sat the flashlight on end, casting a pool of light on the scene.

Margaret's pale face contrasted sharply with the bright red blood trickling down her cheek; the dried blood on the side of her head was a darker hue. I'd gotten a good look at the area earlier, but now I examined it more closely. She was on her back, a cut next to her eye, matted blood extending into her hairline. If she'd tripped and fallen, I'd expect to see a lump on her temple, maybe a cut as well, but not a gash. How had that gotten there? I raised the lantern, illuminating a wider area, and saw nothing that might have caused the wound. Whatever had been used wasn't here. Someone had taken it with them, or she'd been attacked someplace else and brought here.

Hensley had stopped moving or making any sounds.

Corrigan checked her wrist. "I feel a pulse, but it's faint."

"Michael, I think she was struck with something."

"I was thinking the same thing."

Detectives Nelson and Rodriguez stepped into the passageway. Scott remained at the doorway.

"Scott," Corrigan said, "bring a couple of blankets."

"Got it," he replied and left.

Corrigan and I stood, got out of the detectives' way, and went to the laundry room.

We looked at each other in the momentary lull.

"Michael . . ." I shook my head. "Whatever is this madness about?"

"I wish I knew." His ruddy complexion was redder than usual. "Better yet, I wish I could get my hands on whoever is behind it."

Scott came back with blankets, and Corrigan took them into the passageway. I told Scott what we'd seen and what we suspected. A siren wailed in the distance.

Scott put his arm around my shoulders and gave me a gentle hug. "More reason than ever for you to be careful. Michael told me about his plans and what he wants you to do. Promise you'll always have someone you can count on nearby until this is over."

"Promise," I replied. No more buts like the ones in my earlier conversation. The attack on me and then Hensley in the same day could mean the murderer was getting more desperate.

The siren grew louder, and Scott stepped out of the door to wave them over. The wailing stopped and two paramedics rushed in.

"She's in there," I said, pointing to the hallway.

They went in and Corrigan came out. "I'm getting my keys so I can follow them to the hospital. Scott, I want you to escort Kelly to the B and B."

"Shall do."

An EMT ran by and returned with a gurney. A few minutes later, he and the other one passed by us with Margaret, and shortly thereafter the siren started up again.

Detective Rodriguez emerged, his mouth set in a firm line, corners turned downward. He questioned me about finding Margaret, and I told him what had happened.

"Did you remove anything from the scene?"

"No."

"Did you see anyone in here or nearby?"

"No." I paused. "Do you think it was an accident?" I hoped he'd say yes, but I didn't hold my breath.

"We can't tell for sure," Detective Rodriguez answered. "Unlikely, though, Ms. Jackson. Mr. Corrigan has asked me to spend the night at your inn for protection purposes. I'll be over later."

"All right. Scott's going to follow me there now."

The detective nodded and went back in the passageway. Picking up my purse, I went with Scott out the back door to where our vehicles were parked. I got in my truck and started home, with Scott behind me in the mansion's Cadillac. When we got there, we went up the back steps together. Gazing through the window, I saw Helen in the kitchen and Stevie walking by with a cup in his hand. I knew from the gold Mercedes in the parking lot the Silver Sentinels had arrived.

"I'm going to join Corrigan at the hospital," Scott said. "Call if you need anything . . . and be careful."

"I will."

He gazed at me for a few moments, then started down the steps. Entering the multipurpose room, I found it alive with activity. Tommy was practicing his presentation to an enthralled audience of three dogs, Allie, and Stevie, who'd turned his chair around and rested his arms on the back of it.

Tommy pointed to a picture on his trifold board. "This is a gray whale." Three dog tails pounded the floor. "And this is a tube worm, one of the many things they eat." More dog claps. Allie and Stevie nodded encouragingly.

Helen was putting spoonfuls of dough on a cookie sheet. "Hi, Kelly." She stopped, washed her hands, and came over to me. "Are you okay?" she whispered. "Mr. Corrigan asked me to set up a room for you and one for a detective, but he didn't tell me why."

"Let's go in the study," I said.

As we walked down the hallway, Helen said, "I put the two of you in the rooms at the head of the stairs."

I closed the door. "I'm okay. There was an incident, and it involves the police. They've asked me not to talk about it for now." I decided not to mention what happened to Hensley. It would only make Helen worry more.

"I'll sure be glad when this is over," Helen said.

"That makes two of us." I changed the subject as we headed back. "Tommy has an enthusiastic audience."

Helen smiled. "Yes. I'm going to listen to him when he feels he's got it perfected."

We entered the workroom.

"The Silver Sentinels are in the conference room," Helen said. "They told me you are joining them for dinner."

"Yes. A chance to plan our next steps."

Helen went back to her cookies just as Daniel entered with a large pizza box.

"Oh, boy! Pizza!" Tommy's presentation came to an abrupt end.

I left them to their dinner and went to see the Sentinels. The room was filled with a delicious aroma.

Gertie stood at a large pot, ladling hot steaming soup into a bowl. "Hi, Kelly. Glad you could join us. Come over and get some minestrone soup. I made it with vegetables from my garden. I thought something healthy was in order after all the rich food we ate today."

The others greeted me as they got their plates and soup and settled at the table. A basket of homemade wheat bread was in the center.

Joining them, I took the proffered bowl. "Smells wonderful, Gertie."

Green beans, carrots, and numerous other vegetables mixed in with pasta shells and kidney beans swirled as I stirred the soup. I took a sip and found the ingredients provided a great combination of flavors in the rich broth.

Taking another spoonful, I said, "And it tastes as good as it smells."

Mary presented a pie, rounding out the meal. "I decided on apple so we could be sure to have our fruit for the day."

The Professor put a slice of bread on his plate. "Anything new in the investigation, Kelly?"

I told them what had happened and what I knew about Hensley and Robert Johnson, alias Robert James, but kept my word to Deputy Sheriff Stanton about not mentioning what had happened to me. I didn't see any way they could help with that, and it would only upset them.

"Let's review what we have so far," I suggested. "We're proceeding on the theory the attack on Gertie and Sylvia's murder are connected because of the hatpins from the mansion, and we are searching for someone from Redwood Heights. Based on the size of the person, as best Gertie and Stevie could tell, we had five suspects: Hensley, Lily Wilson, Tina Smith, Jerry Gershwin, and Robert James."

Rudy listed the names on a chart.

"I'd dropped Jerry off because he had an alibi, then he lost it, now he's got his alibi back." I filled them in and received some chuckles over his Meat King title. "We can cross him off the list."

The Professor said, "I believe Hensley should be eliminated as well. It's highly unlikely there's more than one person behind this. I think we should go with what's most feasible first. If we don't get our answers there, we can start on a new round of suspects."

Rudy drew a red line through Hensley's name.

Gertie turned down the hot plate the soup rested on and joined us at the table. "Since Hensley's was the most recent incident, why don't we start there with our next steps?"

Mary was cutting her pie. "Oh, good idea. We could find out when was the last time someone saw her."

"I saw lady when we go see Kelly at the event," Ivan volunteered.

Rudy started a new chart labeled timeline. "That was about two thirty."

"I don't remember when I last saw her," I said. "The afternoon's a blur. But maybe some of the others working there will."

The Professor helped himself to a piece of pie. "Two of the suspects were working there—Lily and Tina. We could ask what people remembered about their whereabouts during the event, as well as Margaret Hensley's."

"Phil and Andy might wonder why we are asking about those two. The others already know about our suspect list. I think it's time we tell them what we know and what we're planning," I said. "It might put a different light on what they think to tell us."

The Sentinels nodded agreement.

"We'll be interviewing Tina and Lily," Rudy said, "as part of our gathering information about the manager. That might give us some clues as to what they were doing."

"I agree," I said. "But I believe you should continue to work in pairs."

"I'm happy to talk to Lily," Mary said. "We've done community work together. She worked as a nurse and goes with me when I deliver food to needy members in the community and talks to them about their health."

"I'll go with you," Rudy said. "I've talked with Lily a couple of times at town hall meetings."

"I can do Tina," Gertie said. "I really enjoyed the raw food appetizers today and asked her lots of questions. We connected, and I told her she could have some vegetables from my garden."

"I go with," Ivan said. "We a pair on this case."

"That leaves Michael, Andy, Phil, Daniel, and Scott who were working the event." I paused.

"I volunteer for Phil and Andy and telling them about our suspicions," the Professor said.

"I'll talk to Michael, Scott, and Daniel." I pointed to the suspect list. "There are two more names we can add—the CEO, Mark Benton, and his sister, but I'd put them off to the side. I don't know their size, which is part of the criteria for our list. I'll check with Michael."

Rudy frowned as he wrote their names. "Why would you include them? They didn't stay at the mansion."

"No, but he and his sister would've had access to it at some point since they were going to buy it. They might've met Sylvia," I said.

"We haven't figured out how the person got the hatpins," Gertie said. "Lily or Tina might have found a way since they are on staff and live on site, but how would the others manage it?"

"The key appeared new," I said, "definitely not the original that came with the cabinet. There could've been a number of duplicates made and they found a way to get one. Robert Johnson is a billionaire—he has a billion ways to influence people to give him what he wants."

Mary piped up. "Maybe the buyers asked for keys to get a closer look at some of the items. They could've kept that one 'accidentally' or had a copy made."

"Excellent thought, Mary," Gertie said.

"We don't have a motive yet for the murder or the attack on Hensley," the Professor said. "What's driving all of this?"

I spoke up. "Robert Johnson really wants the property. You could hear it in his voice and see it in his eyes. If Sylvia made the connection to who he was, the deal would have been dead right then and there."

"Had he met Sylvia?" the Professor asked.

"He said no, but obviously he's not above lying," I said.

Gertie chimed in. "Maybe the CEO thought the money sounded better than doing his own development after all."

Mary put her fork down. "Maybe Sylvia pushed Tina or Lily too far, and they were concerned about losing their jobs."

"Those are all possibilities, but how does the attack on Hensley fit in?" *Or me.* "I don't have a clue. We'll have to keep gathering information until something comes to light."

The Professor said, "Sounds like we have our new direction and our assignments. Maybe tomorrow will take us to the killer."

Noticing the pitcher was empty, I picked it up. "I'll get some more water."

I went to the main room and started to fill the container from the water cooler.

Helen came over and handed me a note. "I forgot to give this to you earlier."

Henrietta, Henry as she liked to be called, had phoned collect. The message said she had more information but not to call after nine, which was six o'clock here. It had been too late to call by the time I got to the inn. I knew what I'd be doing in the morning.

"Thanks, Helen."

I gazed around the room. The kids and the dogs were playing, while Stevie and Daniel watched television. Helen's cookies had filled the room with mouthwatering smells. I'd be so happy when this was the routine instead of talking about tracking down a murderer.

Henry had called. She wouldn't do that for a social reason. What had she found out? Would it be something that would lead us to the answer we so desperately needed?

Chapter 25

Helen answered a knock on the door and opened it for Detective Rodriguez. We exchanged hellos, decided to meet about seven in the morning, and I said I'd call him when I was ready. Helen gave him his room information, and he excused himself to continue with his paperwork. Daniel and Stevie looked quizzical but went back to watching their show, and I returned to the Sentinels.

Studying our list of our primary suspects, I said, "We have a billionaire, a young woman with a bright future ahead, and a caregiver. It's as clear as mud which one is a murderer."

Ivan wrinkled his brow. "Clear mud? Would like to see."

The Professor smiled. "It's an idiom, Ivan."

"An idiotums?" the big man said, and we all laughed.

"Some of them seem idiotic, that's for sure. The word is idiom," the Professor explained. "It's when words put together in a phrase have a different meaning than what you'd find looking each individual word up in the dictionary. For example, if you say something costs an arm and a leg it means it's very expensive."

"Now Ivan get. Like fish on land."

"Sort of. That one's like a fish out of water," the Professor said.

"Yah, yah. Now I remember. Fish out of water."

We worked together to clean dishes and pack up the food. With promises to have an afternoon meeting tomorrow, we said our good nights.

As I was about to leave, I looked at Robert Johnson's picture again. He was talking to a man, and I wondered if it was the CEO. I decided to call Corrigan.

"Hi, Kelly." Corrigan sounded tired.

"How's Margaret?"

"She has a concussion, but it appears she'll be okay."

"That's good news. Is the man in the picture with Robert Johnson the one who wanted to buy the mansion?"

"Yes. When I saw that, I had an idea what Robert was up to."

"Thanks. That's helpful. The Sentinels and I have put together our next plan of action." I didn't ask him about the last time he saw Hensley or for a description of the buyers—that could wait.

"You've all done a great job so far. I'm glad to hear they're still working on it."

We ended the call with promises to be in touch with any new developments.

Examining the picture more closely, I saw a gray-haired man, maybe in his sixties. There had been a second man in the picture Sylvia showed me, and it could have been him. Hard to tell his height, but at least now we knew what he looked like.

I packed a few things and went to my new room.

I rolled out of bed at six and was ready by seven to go downstairs with Detective Rodriguez. Helen had thoughtfully brought me a thermos of coffee since I didn't have a way to make my own. I was anxious to make my call to Henry.

I phoned the detective, and we met on the landing. "Any new information you can share?" I asked.

He shook his head. "There's nothing new. More of an absence of information—no fingerprints at any of the crime scenes, no weapon so far from yesterday's attack, and nothing useful we can see in the interviews."

"Frustrating," I said.

He nodded in agreement.

"Did Michael Corrigan tell you about the papers I've been working on?"

"Just that you found legal documents regarding a lawsuit from about fifty years ago and that it didn't seem relevant to what was happening now."

"Right. The woman lost the case. I talked to a relative and learned a little more. I missed a call from her yesterday, so I'm going to the office to phone her back."

We entered the kitchen and workroom area. Helen was slicing bananas. A dish of yogurt sat nearby.

Helen pointed to two plates on the counter. "Good morning. Breakfast is ready."

Detective Rodriguez's eyes lit up when he saw the frying pan brimming with scrambled eggs with red and green peppers mixed in. Country-fried potatoes heaped on a plate sat on the counter next to a platter of bacon.

"Looks great, Helen. I'm going to return Henry's call, then I'll be in."

I grabbed a cup of coffee as the detective started filling his plate.

Closing the study door behind me, I hesitated a moment, then locked it. I found a notepad and a pen, settled in behind the oak desk, and dialed Henry's number.

"Evans Residential Care. How may I help you?" a voice asked in well-practiced tones.

"Henrietta Reynolds, please," I replied.

"Just a moment. I'll see if she's available." The woman put me on hold.

After what seemed an eternity, Henry came on the line.

"Henry here. Who are you?" the high-pitched elderly voice demanded.

"Kelly Jackson. How are you?"

"Waste of time talkin' about how I am. What do I need to do to get that reward you talked about?"

"Give me new information about Iris and her family."

"How much is it?"

Right. How much? It didn't exist.

"It's a hundred dollars. Any new information about the Brandon family qualifies you." I rolled my eyes. May this never get out.

"If I'd known it was that much, I would've called sooner."

I willed myself to be patient.

"Do Iris's kids count?" Her voice creaked.

"Sure." I perched on the edge of the chair, pen ready. What did the woman know?

"How do I know you'll send me the money?" Suspicion filled her quavering voice.

"You don't. But I will. And you have nothing to lose," I replied.

Henry's laugh was like the crackling of dry leaves. "Way to go, girl. I like your style, and you're learnin' how to get to the point."

I think I heard the phone squeal as I held it in a stranglehold.

"Ethel called yesterday," Henry declared triumphantly. Silence. She didn't continue.

"Who's Ethel?" I asked.

"My word, girl. Don't you know anything? I thought you were researching this family. Well, doesn't matter." Her breath whistled softly over the phone.

I drew a smiley face on my notepad to have something cheerful to look at.

"She's a relative. I asked her about Iris's kids. It seems the youngest boy was ill almost from the get-go. The two older ones took care of him as long as they could. Had to put him in some home early on. Hard to imagine being in a place like that all your life." Her voice trailed off, ending in a whisper.

What kind of life was Henry living? In my excitement, I hadn't thought about the woman I was talking to, where she was, and what she might be going through. I felt a surge of guilt.

In softer tones I asked, "Do you know what happened to the other two?"

"The boy got into some kind of trouble. Both of 'em moved west, Ethel said. Thought maybe California. Wasn't sure."

"Do you have any idea what the name of the place is where they put their younger brother?"

"Nope. You're talking over thirty years ago."

"What were the names of the children?"

"Don't remember the youngest—didn't see him much. The boy went by Cash and the girl's name was Catherine. Do I get my money?" she asked with a shot of spunk in her reedy voice.

"I'll send it tomorrow. If you find out anything else, give me a call. It's not a one-time reward."

I'd pay it myself. A hundred dollars was a lot, but the information might prove useful, and Henry probably needed it more than I did.

"Okay." Henry's voice suddenly seemed filled with the weight of her years.

"Take care, Henry," I said.

"I always take care of myself," Henry fired back. The line disconnected as she banged the phone down.

I sank back in my chair.

Of the current suspects, Robert Johnson and Lily Wilson could be grandchildren, and Tina could be a great-grandchild. I wasn't sure about the CEO and his sister, but the picture made me think they'd be in the grandchildren category.

I kept circling back to the fact Iris had lost the lawsuit. Why would it make any difference now? I didn't think we were going to find the answer in this line of inquiry, but I decided to stay with it. I had nothing to lose, either . . . except my life, if we didn't get an answer soon.

I went to the conference room and studied the photograph of Johnson and the person who was fronting for him. Their facial structures were quite different from each other. Johnson had a narrow face and the other man had high cheekbones and a wide brow. Then it hit me. Family resemblances sometimes were very strong and passed down through the generations. If one of the suspects was a descendant of Mrs. Brandon, the photographs in the carriage house might give us a clue as to who it was.

I went into the kitchen and sat next to Detective Rodriguez, who was heaping a second helping of potatoes on his plate.

"Learn anything?" he asked.

"A little more about the family. Iris Reynolds, who initiated the lawsuit, had two boys and a girl. One of the boys was in poor health and put in a home. The other two might have moved out here."

"Doesn't seem like you got much to go on."

I put peanut butter on a piece of toast and topped it with raspberry jam. "I know what you mean, but I'd like to go look at the photos of Mrs. Brandon I found in the carriage house. Do you have time to go with me? It won't take long. I'll grab a few and take them into the mansion . . . if that's where I'll be." I remembered my day wasn't my own to plan anymore.

"That works. Nelson and I are working in the interview room. We have all our papers spread out there." He looked at his watch. "I'm meeting him at eight thirty, so I have time to go up there with you. You can come back to the mansion with me until you get your day figured out."

We thanked Helen for breakfast, got our things from our rooms, and headed for Redwood Heights. We parked in back next to each other and walked up the path. When we arrived at the carriage house, I took out the key and started to move the yellow crime scene tape.

Detective Rodriguez stepped beside me. "Let me do that." He took the key, pulled the tape aside, and unlocked the door.

He entered and flipped on the light switch. "You stay behind me."

The first part of the room remained much the same. However, there was a considerable change at the back. The police had broken down a large section of the wall, in order to remove the skeleton. Now one could easily walk into the once-hidden room. The empty carriage sat in the back, a dusty, outdated means of travel, but no longer a casket.

Detective Rodriguez checked behind boxes and inside the carriage. "Looks like the coast is clear."

His phone rang. "Detective Rodriguez." He listened. "What do you mean it's about my wife? Just a minute." He turned to me. "I'm going to take this outside. I'll be at the doorway."

I'd already headed for the box of photographs. "Okay. I'll be out in a few minutes."

Some light now found its way into the room from the newly made opening, but I still needed my flashlight to look at the pictures. I pulled it out and opened the steamer trunk. The stack of photos was still there. I wanted to get a good photo of Mrs. Brandon's face, preferably from different angles, as well as a sense of how tall she was.

One photo had her in a portrait setting, leaning against a fireplace mantel, showing her to be on the tall side. Another gave her facial profile as she petted a horse. Digging deeper, I found one of her facing the camera, dark hair piled high, her eyes challenging and inviting. High cheekbones. Wide eyes. Two people came to mind—the CEO and Lily Wilson.

Violet. Iris. Lily.

Goose bumps erupted on my arms. I'd found the granddaughter. Why had she kept quiet about her family connection? She must be hiding it for a reason.

Had I found the killer?

"Detective Rodriguez," I shouted. I jumped up and turned around—only to find Lily blocking my path.

Chapter 26

Lily's silhouette filled the doorway. She turned and pulled the door closed.

The last time the door had closed, I'd been trapped inside. A prickle of apprehension rippled through me.

Her full skirt reached to the floor, the ebony cloth rustling as she stepped toward me. The high-necked lace bodice and long sleeves extending over the backs of her hands had once protected travelers of the horse and buggy era. A fine black mesh veil from a small-brimmed hat shrouded her features—the apparel of mourning. Lily lifted the delicate fabric with one hand.

"Detective Rodriguez?" I forced his name through my constricted throat.

"He won't be coming," Lily said. "He had to go."

What exactly did she mean by that?

Lily pointed to the items I held in my hands. "I see you have some photographs."

"Yes. I was trying to see if there was a family resemblance to anyone involved with the mansion. I think Mark Benton, the man who wants to buy the mansion, looks somewhat like her."

I had no intention of mentioning her likeness.

She smiled. "As well he should. He's my brother, and we're Brandon descendants. The woman you found in the coach was our grandmother."

Shocked at her admission, I asked, "Lily, why didn't you tell people about your connection to the family?"

Lily sighed. "It was my secret. When I came here, I took a position as a nurse to care for the ailing owners. They were involved in the lawsuit and wouldn't have hired me if they'd known my mother was the one who sued them. I changed my name from Catherine, my paternal grandmother's name, to Lily, which is what my mother felt was in keeping with the Brandon tradition. Wilson was a convenient name on our family tree."

I shifted uneasily.

"I decided if I couldn't own Redwood Heights, maybe I could at least live in it. Mom often showed us pictures of the place." Her face took on a dreamy expression. "I knew every detail of what was in those photographs—the inlaid tables, the crystal chandeliers, the marble fireplaces. It was all to be ours . . . and should be ours."

"Now there's proof there was a child. You can reopen the case."

Lily shook her head. "I saw the pitying looks people gave my mother. They laughed her out of court . . . said she'd forged the birth certificate. Threatened to arrest her . . . the owners with all their money and fancy attorneys. It would be no different now. I watched her waste away and die a little more inside each day. Her affection for my brothers and me shriveled to nothing. Besides, it's too late."

"What do you mean it's too late?"

"The Porter woman, if only she hadn't been such a busybody. My brother saw her taking pictures when he met with Johnson one morning at the mansion. I tried stealing her camera."

The shove on the stairs.

"I planned to make her sick so she'd leave. I brought some pills to work with me. I knew when she showed you the picture and said it was Robert Johnson, I had to do something more. He'd told us the deal wouldn't go through if Corrigan found out he was involved. I couldn't take a chance she'd show it to him or someone who knew of their past."

My eyes searched the room for anything I might be able to use as a weapon.

"That's why I had to silence Hensley, too. She recognized the name and would've remembered the connection in time. A blow to the head kept her out of commission. For Sylvia, I added a little something to her tea." Lily smiled. "She'd wanted to try on some hats. I took one to her room. The drug I gave her worked. She could hardly stand. I helped her to the chair; I pulled out my hatpin and stabbed her. It was so easy. You see, that's why there won't be a new lawsuit. It's too late."

She shifted her position, revealing an aluminum bat she held that had been hidden in the folds of the voluminous skirt.

I stepped back.

Lily glanced at her watch. "The deal would've been done by now." She laughed, a hollow, mirthless sound. "Today would've been the day for me to take my rightful place as lady of the manor. At last, after all these years, I would've slept in my grandmother's room."

Fear rooted me to the ground.

"Instead of getting my rightful inheritance, I ended up emptying bedpans and administering medicine to the pathetic owners. Then later, the tours. I hated having all those strangers traipse through my house."

Her voice got higher pitched and louder. The folds of her skirt whispered together as she stepped toward me.

Her harsh, vehement voice rent the dust-filled air. "First the Porter woman and then you. Messing up my plans. Sticking your nose in where it didn't belong. I tried to scare you away with the fire. If you and those meddling seniors had stayed out of it, I would've been able to live here the rest of my life." Lily raised her arms, bat overhead. "I got rid of her, and I'll get rid of you!"

I threw the framed pictures in Lily's face, turned, and ran. A crash and the tinkle of breaking glass sounded.

"There's nowhere for you to go." Her low, husky whisper was more chilling than her loud rant.

And she was right. There was no place to hide, no way out.

I spied the carriage. The dark eyes of its empty window frames stared at me. I reached it, yanked the door open, and threw myself inside. I slammed the door closed and slid the bolt in place just as Lily grabbed the door.

The handle of the carriage door rattled as she twisted it, but the lock held. The carriage tilted as Lily stood on the step. Her face peered through the door's window, her eyes like smoldering black coals. Her fingers curled over the sill.

Her face disappeared. The bat hit the bottom of the window frame. Wood splinters flew, a few hitting my face. The whole carriage shuddered as another smashing blow hit the door. The thick wood remained intact.

Lily hit the side of the window frame nearest the door. "I will get you," she said through clenched teeth.

The frame began to disintegrate. She was working on the area nearest the handle. If she destroyed enough of the wood panel, she'd be able to reach in and grab the bolt. I tried the door on the other side. Jammed. Probably warped.

I peered out a window next to it. Boxes and trunks blocked the left side below. I could pull myself out through the window, but I'd have to go by Lily to escape the building. I searched around the carriage for anything I could use as a weapon. The dim light showed only the bare interior, disintegrating leather cushions, and a broken sconce.

In the upper corner I spied another wall sconce, this one intact. Maybe that could be used as a weapon. Shaped like a large shell, the glass appeared thick. I didn't want Lily to see what I was doing, so I picked up a cushion and leaned it against the window frame she was smashing. The second seat cushion I placed against the door in case she looked in again.

I reached up and explored the glass cover. How was it connected? The sconces had to be easily removed because they had to be refilled with oil so often. Desperately my fingers searched—shoving, twisting, pulling. I pushed upward, and the glass cover moved. I freed it from its base.

The carriage reverberated from the blows of the bat.

I needed to cover the glass with something to protect myself when I hit her. I cradled my precious cargo under my arm as I tried to unzip my jacket. I tugged at the zipper. It reluctantly went down a few notches. Frantically, I jerked at the zipper. It relented, and I struggled out of the thin jacket and wrapped the sconce.

"I will end this." Lily's voice was low and menacing.

I heard a large intake of breath. A quick glance out the gaping hole to the left of the door showed a twisted face framed by two uplifted arms.

"Now!" Lily's voice, filled with rage, fueled the bat. With strength born from years of hate, Lily smashed the window frame once again, destroying what was left of the wood panel.

She pushed the cushion out of the way, reached in, and unlocked the door. She opened it.

"You can't get away from me." She reached up and grabbed the metal handle next to the right side of the door. "I'm going to kill you." Lily seized the left side of the door frame with her other hand, managing to hold on to the bat. She began pulling herself into the carriage, her features contorted like some primitive mask.

I rose as high as I could and, using both hands, hit her right temple with all of my strength with the sconce. She lost her grip on the door and fell forward into the carriage. She didn't lose her hold on the bat. She shook her head from side to side, as if to clear her mind. It was the best I could hope for. The glass had shattered from the force of the blow. The sconce had done its job. I dropped it. It was of no further use.

I spun around and went to the window. Putting my back against the windowsill, I grasped the top of the frame with both hands and pulled myself out, my back scraping against the rough wood. I dropped among the dark shapes of trunks and boxes and turned to my right. I crouched at the back of the coach and peered around the corner. Lily was still slumped forward.

I lunged past her as she righted herself. She reached out and grabbed my arm. I jerked it away and continued to run. I heard heavy breathing behind me. I wouldn't make it to the door. I needed another weapon. I'd seen gardening equipment along the side wall and sprinted to that area. I snatched an iron rake and turned. Lily was almost upon me.

I swung my rake at her bat; our equipment became our swords. We hit several times, the bat pinging when it hit the metal. I had the advantage of distance, but her bat was stronger. My grip loosened on the handle as she nailed it with a hard blow.

I needed to do something different before I lost the rake.

I rammed the end of it into her stomach then swung the rake tooth side out into the arm holding the bat.

Lily screamed as the metal cut through her sleeve. Her hand went to the wound. She dropped the bat, staggered back, and stepped onto the hem of her long dress. She toppled over and then struggled to untangle herself from all the fabric.

I didn't wait to see if she was successful. Her fall gave me the few precious seconds I needed. I ran.

Then I remembered the two additional wedges I'd found earlier. I grabbed them from the floor near the door, wrenched it open, and plunged outside. Slamming it shut, I shoved one wedge and then the other under the door.

The bat smashed into the wood. Once . . . then again. It held.

Lily shouted, "Let me out!"

I knew only too well how effective those triangular pieces of wood were.

Chapter 27

I sat back on the ground and took in deep gulps of air, getting my breath back. Lily smashed the door again. I looked around for Detective Rodriguez. He was struggling to sit up, a hand to his head, by the side of the building.

"Kelly!" I recognized Scott's voice. I turned to see him, Detective Nelson, and Deputy Sheriff Stanton running toward me. The detective went to his partner, and Stanton pulled out his gun.

Scott knelt beside me. "Are you okay?"

"Yes," I replied. "Just a few scratches."

"What's going on?" Stanton asked.

"Lily's the one who killed Sylvia." It had gotten quiet. "She's in the carriage house with an aluminum bat."

Stanton nodded and went to the door.

"I have it jammed," I told him.

He bent down, removed the wedges, and said, "Lily Wilson, Deputy Sheriff Stanton here. Come out with your hands up."

Silence.

He repeated his request.

Detective Nelson joined him. "Paramedics are on the way."

Stanton opened the door and entered cautiously. Scott and I stood at the doorway as the men searched behind trunks and covered furniture.

I had a hunch I knew where she was. "Deputy Stanton, try the carriage."

The men walked over to it, and I heard Stanton say, "Lily, come out with your hands in sight."

"I'm sitting where my grandmother sat," Lily replied. "I can almost feel her presence."

"Lily, we've known each other for a long time. You've done some good things in the community and helped others. Don't make this difficult."

Lily stepped out and turned to look at the carriage. She traced the coat of arms with a finger. "It was finally going to be mine, all mine, to live in the rest of my life," she crooned. Dust covered her once-pristine black dress, and it was ripped in several places. The hat had vanished, and her hair fell in twisted strands around her shoulders.

In a swift movement, Stanton grabbed her arms, pulled them behind her back, and cuffed her.

The officers escorted her out. Scott and I stared at the demolished panel between the window and the door—jagged edges of wood like shark's teeth protruding from the frame.

"A lot of rage behind those blows," I said. "It gave her super strength."

"I'm glad none of them landed on you." He paused and stared at me. "They didn't, did they? You're not keeping something from me, are you?"

"No. I was able to keep away from her."

"I'm so glad." He nodded his head toward the door. "Let's go."

Outside, the paramedics were talking to a now-standing Detective Rodriguez, telling him he needed to go to the hospital to be checked out.

"I will," he assured them. He spotted me. "Ms. Jackson, are you okay?"

"Yes. How are you?"

"Lucky," replied one of the EMTs.

"That I am," the detective said. "I began to get suspicious about the call. The person put me on hold. I heard a noise and turned. She got me, but not as bad as she could've."

His partner joined him. "Nah, it was your hard head that saved you."

Scott and I walked back together, and I told him what had happened. As we arrived at the mansion, Deputy Sheriff Stanton drove out with Lily in the back of his cruiser. Her back was ramrod straight—a proud Brandon.

"What brought you and the others up to the carriage house?" I asked.

"Detective Nelson said it was very unusual for his partner to be late. When he called him, Rodriguez didn't answer. With all that's been happening, we decided to come up and check."

I stopped by my truck. "It's over. What a relief."

And it meant my life could get back to my new normal.

Scott took out his phone. "I'm going to call Corrigan."

"And I'm going home to wash up and change."

"Okay."

I saw Stevie and his four-legged kids in the distance walking the perimeter of a building and waved. I went over and told him the news and that Gertie was now safe. He took out his phone to call her, and I asked him to have her notify the others of the turn of events.

When I got home, I decided to go in the side door, wanting some time to myself. I walked into my place and stopped to take in the sparkling ocean, the gulls swooping by the window, uttering their distinctive cries, and the lush garden dotted with a myriad of colorful flowers. Peace settled on me like a soft cloak.

I checked my face in the bathroom mirror and found a few minute scratches where splinters had grazed the skin. My fingers were a little worse than they had been earlier after my last visit to the carriage house, and my back had some red lines. That was it. I was lucky, too.

Scott called and said Corrigan and the officers wanted to meet at three thirty in the interview room at the mansion and asked me to invite the Silver Sentinels.

I called the Professor. "It's over. We know who killed Sylvia."

"So I heard," he said. "We were assembling so we could come over and remove the murder investigation charts and set up for the original task you assigned us . . . if you still want us to do that."

I'd forgotten about the boxes of newspaper clippings and photos. "Absolutely, Professor."

Nice. That would keep my friends close by. I told him about the meeting.

"Delighted to join in. See you then," he responded. "I'll alert the others."

I went to the multipurpose room and found Helen making a grocery list. I filled her in on the parts of the story she didn't know. She was as relieved as the rest of us. She shared that Tommy and Allie were working in the cottage next door and would be over later.

"That is, if it's okay with you, Kelly. I don't know how you feel about them feeling free to come and go in here."

Helen and I hadn't had much time to talk about my new status or the operation of the inn.

"I love having them here. We're a family—the Redwood Cove Bed-and-Breakfast family."

Helen appeared relieved. "I'm glad you feel that way. I know they really like you."

"The feeling is mutual."

I spent the afternoon reviewing office paperwork and putting finishing touches on settling into my quarters. The Sentinels came by and cleaned up their notes, all smiles and happy chatter.

At the appointed time, I drove to the mansion and parked next to Daniel's truck. People were seated around the large table. Tina and Cindy were each placing a tray of appetizers on it. I saw a pitcher of iced tea and one of water on the sideboard along with glasses. After pouring some tea, I sat next to Gertie.

Deputy Sheriff Stanton and the detectives were there. Detective Rodriguez's hand strayed to the back of his head every so often, probably to check the lump that was surely there.

Another person entered the room: Robert Johnson. I shot a glance at Corrigan, but his face showed no sign of emotion. The newcomer sat at the far end of the table.

Corrigan cleared his throat. "Thank you for coming. As a result of the hard work you all put into this investigation, we have a resolution. Deputy Sheriff Stanton, Detective Nelson, Detective Rodriguez, and I have a few pieces of information you should know to bring closure . . . and I want to make you aware of a decision I've made."

I wondered what he meant by that.

Detective Nelson shuffled some papers in front of him. "Lily's brother, the CEO Mark Benton, had no idea what Lily had done. At least that's what he says, and we have no reason to doubt him."

"Henry said his name was Cash. Did she make a mistake?" I asked.

"No. He'd had problems with the law and decided to change his name when he moved out here," Deputy Stanton replied.

Detective Rodriguez rubbed his neck. "We found a number of prescription bottles belonging to other people at Lily's place. Some of them were from the owners who recently died and made up the final piece of property Mr. Johnson wanted."

Deputy Sheriff Stanton chimed in. "One was supposedly a suicide and the other an accidental overdose. We're going to check into those deaths more closely in case Lily had a hand in them."

"We found the two boxes taken from your vehicle," Detective Nelson said. "Lily heard you mention what you'd found. She didn't think it would impact her but figured it wouldn't hurt to try to get them just in case."

"Sylvia's camera, purse, and necklace were there as well," Detective Rodriguez added.

"Why was the hatpin there when I found Sylvia and then gone later?" I asked.

Deputy Sheriff Stanton said, "I can answer that one. Lily seemed proud of what she'd done, almost bragged about all she'd accomplished, and told us everything."

I shook my head at the thought of how twisted a mind could become.

Stanton continued, "Lily had been wearing the pin that morning and realized it might implicate her. During one of the breaks in the tour, she went back and got it, using the hidden passageway. It was a gamble, but one she won."

"Turns out Lily made good use of the sporting equipment for the guests." Rodriguez looked at me. "That's where the bat came from as well as the croquet mallet she used on Margaret Hensley."

"Why the attack on Gertie?" asked the Professor.

Stanton answered. "Her brother had seen her taking pictures with her phone when he was meeting with Robert Johnson. She was photographing Allie's lunch celebration, and they were in the background. He mentioned it to Lily. She was concerned it might create a problem for her plans . . . which it did, thanks to your excellent sleuthing."

It was nice to hear the deputy give the Sentinels a compliment.

"Thank you, Billy," Gertie said to Deputy Sheriff Bill Stanton.

Rodriguez and Nelson raised their eyebrows.

Gertie replied to their unspoken question. "Billy was in my fifth grade class."

The men chuckled.

Corrigan slid a glass back and forth in front of himself. "About the decision I've made." He looked at Robert Johnson. "Robert, our feud played a role in Sylvia Madison's death. If I hadn't made the pledge to never sell you a piece of property, you wouldn't have had to use deceit to try to buy this place."

Johnson nodded. "What took place has been on my mind as well. If I hadn't tried to trick you, this wouldn't have happened."

"You won't have reason to be tempted again," Corrigan said. "We can deal at the table like two businessmen. If we can come to an agreement about a piece of property, you can buy it. It was silly of me anyway. As soon as I sell a place, someone can turn around and sell it to whomever they want."

"Does that mean you're willing to reconsider about selling this place to me?"

"Perhaps. Let's let a little time pass before we go down that path."

"How is Margaret Hensley?" asked Mary.

"She'll make a full recovery. As soon as she's well, she's returning to New York." Corrigan smiled. "Sylvia Madison's report said Hensley was doing an outstanding job and recommended pictures be taken to use as examples for our staff website."

"Who's going to manage Redwood Heights?" Daniel asked.

"Scott's going to stay until the regular manager returns, which will be in about three weeks." Corrigan glanced around the room. "Anyone have any further questions?"

All heads shook in a negative response.

"I don't have a question, but I do have something to share," I said. "The best way to do that is with a demonstration." I spoke to Mary. "I'd like you to help me."

"Of course, honey, just tell me what you want me to do."

"We're going to take a walk to the far end of the room," I replied.

As we made our way, I asked her to tell me in a quiet voice the ingredients of her brownies when we got to a certain spot. I'd let her know when. She looked puzzled but nodded in agreement.

When we got to the corner of the room, I stopped, looked back, and then shifted where we were standing about a foot so we were in line with the detectives on the other side of the room.

"Now," I said.

She tilted her head to the side. "The recipe calls for chopped pecans, semi-sweet chocolate—"

"What the . . ." Detective Nelson's voice said in my ear.

Mary's head jerked up, and she looked around for the person who had spoken.

We walked back, and I asked Detective Nelson what he'd heard.

"Something about pecans and chocolate. What just happened?"

"Clever, Kelly," the Professor said. "Scientific eavesdropping!"

"Oh, what fun!" Mary said. "Can you tell us about it, Professor?"

"It has to do with the elliptical ceiling and concave shape."

We all stared at the ceiling—the revealer of secrets.

"Sound travels across it. The phenomenon has been known for centuries. It's sometimes referred to as a whispering gallery. A famous, or infamous one, as the case may be, was in the Cathedral of Girgenti in Sicily. The secrets of the confessional traveled approximately two hundred and fifty feet to a spot where even whispers were easily heard. As you can imagine, this caused great dismay on the part of those supposedly speaking in private and sharing their sins."

I spoke to the detectives. "When I was waiting for you to interview me, I sat where you are now. I was surprised when your voices sounded like you were standing right next to me."

"So you heard everything we said?" Rodriguez asked.

"Yes, until you started walking toward me." I smiled at them. "I wanted you to know in case you ever had a ceiling like this above you again."

"We appreciate it," Nelson said ruefully. "Life's full of surprises."

Mary's eyes sparkled. "This could be useful in our investigations. We'll have to see what other places have a ceiling like this."

Corrigan addressed the group. "Anything else?"

Everyone shook their heads.

"Thanks for coming." He stood, then said, "Oh, Kelly, good news. I received word the renovation's complete at Redwood Cove B and B. You're in business."

The Silver Sentinels clapped.

Ivan boomed, "Welcome, new manager!"

We said our good-byes and went our separate ways. Scott was staying for a while. It would be nice to get to know him better, without the tension of a murder case surrounding us.

I drove to Redwood Cove Bed-and-Breakfast, parked, turned off the engine, and sat in the truck for a few minutes thinking about how

I'd driven here listening to the song "Walking on Sunshine." The gray clouds that had covered the happy return had now dissipated.

What I found when I entered the multipurpose room made me smile. Allie and Tommy were taking turns tossing pieces of popcorn to Fred, Jack, and Jill.

Tommy shouted, "Fred won. Five for five."

Fred did a basset hound dance.

"What does he get for winning?" I asked.

Tommy looked puzzled for a few minutes, then grinned. "More popcorn!"

Helen was folding napkins and stacking them on the counter.

"Good news, Helen. I just found out we're officially open for business."

"Great! I'll start stocking up on supplies."

I went to my room, put my purse away, and then went to the conference room. It was back to being a meeting room for ordinary tasks—no longer a place to strategize about finding a murderer.

Rejoining the group in the work area, I found Daniel and Tommy wrestling on the floor, with the dogs jumping into the fray at every available opportunity. Stevie and Allie had pulled out the beanbag chairs and were watching television. I heard a voice from the television call out, "Lassie," and a dog bark.

This was the life I'd wanted to see and be a part of. The phone rang.

I answered it. "Redwood Cove Bed-and-Breakfast. How may I help you?"

"We've been admiring the rooms on your website. Is the one named The Study available tomorrow and the day after?"

"Let me check." I opened the registration book. "Yes, it is." I prepared to write their information in it. My first registration as official manager of Redwood Cove Bed-and-Breakfast.

My new beginning.

ABOUT THE AUTHOR

Janet Finsilver and her husband live in the San Francisco Bay Area. She loves animals and has two dogs—Kylie and Ellie. Janet enjoys horseback riding, snow skiing, and cooking. She is currently working on her next Redwood Cove mystery. Readers can visit her website at: www.janetfinsilver.com

Made in the USA
Middletown, DE
08 July 2016